D*E*DALUS

First published in 2018 by Henningham Family Press.
130 Sandringham Road, London, E8 2HJ
henninghamfamilypress.co.uk
@HenninghamPress

All rights reserved

© Chris McCabe, 2018

The right of Chris McCabe to be identified
as author of this work has been asserted in accordance
with the Copyright, Designs & Patents Act 1988

Illustrations © David Henningham, 2018

Printed and bound by T.J. International Ltd, Padstow
& Henningham Family Press, London

ISBN 9781999797423
EPUB 9781999797461
ARTISTS' BOOK (henninghamfamilypress.co.uk)

D*E*DALUS

Chris McCabe

HENNINGHAM FAMILY PRESS

London

2018

for James Joyce

'What's the matter now?'

Hamlet

CONTENTS

PART I

Telemachus: *Act 1, Scene 1*	1
Nestor: *Act 1, Scene 2*	9
Act 1, Scene 3	15
Proteus: *Act 1, Scene 4*	23

PART II

Calypso: *Act 1, Scene 5*	41
Lotus Eaters: *Act 2, Scene 1*	51
Hades: *Act 2, Scene 2*	59
Aeolus: *Act 3, Scene 1*	67
Lestrygonians: *Act 3, Scene 2*	71
Scylla and Charybdis: *Act 3, Scene 3*	79
Wandering Rocks: *Act 3, Scene 4*	87
Sirens: *Act 4, Scene 1*	95
Cyclops: *Act 4, Scene 2*	107
Nausicaa: *Act 4, Scene 3*	113
Oxen of the Sun: *Act 4, Scene 4*	119
Circe: *Act 4, Scene 5*	137

PART III

Eumaeus: *Act 4, Scene 6*	165
Act 4, Scene 7	177
Ithaca: *Act 5, Scene 1*	183
Penelope: *Act 5, Scene 2*	197

NOTES	*219*

Part I

TELEMACHUS

Act 1, Scene 1: Elsinore. A platform before the castle / the Martello Tower. 8am

His wet trousers clung to the back of the chair, slack legs swinging. Seasand and airdew. Those trousers which were not his own. Bracken on his breeks. Along the dawnblue bay he'd walked back from Bloom's, and mishearing his name the name had stuck : *Leonard*. Stephen thought sleepily of the silent couple asleep in a doubledream of catpurrs and silences. In the sourbreath of parental love.

Leonard. Good Samaritan, pockets lined with sumac. Greasy nose. Exposed offal. That kindness of the Biblical innkeeper. Sadness frothing from his eyes like overboiled eggwhites. His wife a regular Lilith. Mattress like a compactus on her back. Was it a stage for me to enter into, adulterous? Perhaps he wanted me to watch? Could have saved money in Monto.

Stephen tried to lift himself up from the bed. The room spun in a circuit of lights like a sun caught in an oculus. His tousled head burrowed the shameconcealing pillow. The incident with the chandelier. Rage of the prostitute. Gnashing Succubus. Good job Leonard was there to pick up the fragments.

A clattering rose up the staircase. Breakfast. Stench of Irish Bacon, cooked arseways. Aftertaste of the rind. Haines, the bastard. And Mulligan : after lending him the quid too.

Friday's children would be fattening like seals across the sand, on their way to class. Black liquorice teeth. Loving and giving under the whalefeed of the clouds. He had to teach.

There was a taste on his tongue redolent of ash. His mother's womb, cornground. A nerve flickered in his cheek like the endwick of a candle. Before him she rose, noseless and whitehaired : his bookshelf still perceptible behind her lucent form. Afterglow of absinthe : look away. A trick of consciousness, conscience. Out damned spot. Back into the snuffjar.

He turned over, pulling the pillow across his face. Horatio's doubt : Tush, tush, 'twill not appear. Your ghost precedes the action. Ho, ratio : he laughs at reason. Ded, alus : I've been turned to stone with over-consumption. Thou art a scholar; speak to it, Horatio.

EXIT GHOST.

Scent of Bass ale, absinthe and cabman's smoke bled into the weltering cotton. A plate clattered downstairs. Outside, the sea collapsed its ceramic frills along the cove. Boody, Dilly, Katey, Maggy : their stomach's hollow tureens. He'd shake the imprint of Monto and pass on his winnings. Wait until father goes on his tavern-trawl, dillydallyingdancingdedalus.

Outside a gull shrieked its Mr Punch across the rocks. Its wingspan momentarily blacked out the sunlight. Massive hearts they are said to have. Pulsing reverb through hollow bones.

He rose in bed : his stomach contracted inside its dry canvas. Aristotle, the body-giver. Walking the beach in exegesis, attempting to unsex the skeleton : the day had collapsed in the curling fumes of liquor. Overthought followed by amnesia.

Ah, his mother. Poor mother, her flesh a potpourri of white ashes. She was with him more completely now that she was nomore. In the mastication of her extremities. What next? If I can't shake her will I need the shock of exorcism? He looked at the book on his dresser : William James, *The Will to Believe and Other Essays in Popular Philosophy*. Another of his Parisian indulgences, like the lemon Mulligan had mocked in his tea. *Therapia*, from the Greek *Therapeia*; curing, healing, service done for the sick : a waiting on. I have made a Fortinbras of she who bore me. *Extorted treasure in the womb of earth.*

School first. Must shake this mordant aftertaste.

He lifted his trousers from the back of the chair : they rattled, heavy with loose coins. Glory for the winged winner. Throwaway, Pegasus of the turf. Kept it chestwise. Kinch the concealer. Gave half-a-crown to Cordroy, must remember. Round of absinsthes. Should I have told? Judas of the turf. No, not between a funeral and a birth. More gold in my cup.

An apple sat squat on the dresser, tucked inside its tight green jacket. Should have took it yesterday. Teacher's gift. Three black mouths had grown from it, like warts. He tried to bite them : the pressure on his teeth seethed sharply in pain. Must see someone for these mental problems : slip of the tongue. *Dental.* The mouth that conceals reveals. The mouth of Chrysostomos isn't gold but red and green.

He put the apple back. Bitemarks quickly yellowing. Fleshbruises. He rolled up his shirtsleeve, slack on thin arms : a blueblack kidney flagged his shoulderblade. A bruise from nighttown. The fight of Mabbot Street. A mnemonic from the whores.

He slipped the stale dollyrag of yesterday's shirt over his pinched frame. Blood, or Portugese port, plumed the cuffs. He walked from his room to the cool stonehead of the staircase. The sound of a spoon clinkclattering the ceramic edge of a cup rose up the stairs.

Stephen descended, his leaden stomach one step behind him on each stair. He entered the kitchen : a lone form sat at the table, back turned to him. A cottager in his homeland. Haines.

Stephen spoke :

– I to sulphurous and tormenting flames must render up myself.
– You suffer?
– I do. I fear there is disloyalty under my roof.
– By which you mean?
– I was not *compos mentis*. You and Mulligan abandoned me there.
– The night train from Westland Row Station was leaving. The absinthe I fear had left its legacy.
– You took my drink then took leave of me.

– I am here to learn your culture, not to nanny it ...

Silence. Stephen sat, then spoke :

– Can you pass me the milk?

Stephen lifted the jug of yesterday's milk to whiten the bronze platitudes of the tea. It splashed the surface in clotted chunks.

– I refuse to live here anymore. Where is Mulligan?
– He left for his morning swim.
– He was already drowning in the stagnation of drink.
– Six o'clock he was up, doing pressups on the balcony.
– He has the heart of an ox. Like yours it pumps Saxon blood.
– And yours?
– Limescale and dungmoss. I have passed the midpoint of life.

A cat clawed cleanly in the door, stretched, and walked on circuspaws to circle the feet of the men. Haines tried to throw down the rindfat from his bacon : it stuck to his finger like ragworm. The cat took it neat to its back teeth and chewed. Its angular otter's head turned obliquely : working the jaw in vociferous knots. Stephen spoke :

– I am surprised with your comfort around this feline?
– By which you are referring to my dream of the panther?

– By which I mean your fear of this country.

Haines bent down to stroke the arched back of the underfed cat :

– All except you have made me welcome here.

Stephen poured more tea into his mug. His pliant hands refused to stifle an exaggerated yawn, his small feminine mouth widened, exposing the pink hull of his palate. He spoke quietly :

– My sisters grow thin on potatoes and margarine.
– And so?
– You allowed this milk to sour.
– We took breakfast together yesterday. I am only one third responsible.

Stephen rose and reached for the ashplant, the coatstand's mirrored spine. He lifted, stopped to blow his nose, and walked to descend the ladder to the beach. He looked up at the fortress he must flee from. *Omphalos* Mulligan had called it. How so? Built by the English in fear of a one-armed tyrant. History casts its shadow.

COCK CROWS.

Haines stared across the table as Stephen, agitated, switched from Shakespeare to Dante :

– And lo! Almost where the ascent began, A panther light and swift exceedingly swift.
– Dante?
– He does. A country he has defined.
– He drew heavily on Virgil.
– That is the musing of a pleasure reader.
– He was not, like Shakespeare, an original.
– Shakespeare never had an idea in his life. His stories were plucked.
– You will agree, though, that he has not been surpassed?
– He will remain unsurpassed for ten years.

Haines drained the last of his cup. Stephen teased :

– A panther light.
– You will not let me forget?
– Dante began his epic with a panther, so shall I.

As if to add flourish to his words Stephen turned his back to Haines and with the dancer's nimbleness descended the stairs. The morning, in russet mantle clad, led him foot-by-foot to the tepid beach.

NESTOR

Act 1, Scene 2: A room of state in the castle / the Forty Foot, Sandycove. 9.30am

An otter's head skimmed landwards and peeled back a rosepink underside : Mulligan. Stephen caught his scornwet eyes and waited. His stomach bit. Mulligan's head dipped and resurfaced. Silver rivulets of water raced along his plumpwet frame. Wellfed jowls smiled back at him :

– The Prince has risen!

The tart sandwet taste of the sea rose to Stephen's senses. He took an indraught and coughed. Mulligan ran boyishly to the tide as Stephen sat. He spat drily into the mudflat. Beside him two winged ants walked in unison. He looked : the male had pinned the hindwings of the female to itself and was walking it where it would.

Across the bay Stephen watched two lithe young men walk citywards, a scroll held like a torchlight was in the hand of the tallest. Cornelius and Voltimand walking from the frame of their fifteen seconds, heading towards Norwegian waters.

A crab crawled across Stephen's boot : he flicked it with his ashplant. It landed backdown on Mulligan's towel. Its white branchroots cluttered amongst its armour. Stephen watched the creature's futile breaststroke. Mulligan reached for the towel and made a cloak around his shoulders.

– Kinch! We looked for you all around ...
– I was unable to move.
– We waited. Your friend, the Jew, was very close to you.

The crab crawled sideways along the doctor's broad left shoulder. Stephen watched its performance : a comedian with eight walking sticks, commanding a silent screen. That constellation, cancer, that ate my mother. Her exoskeleton rising on her face. *Beastly dead*, he had called her.

Mulligan bent and stroked the starched towel along one leg, then another, dry. The crab held rank on his sunflanked shoulder. Elsinore. A platform before the castle. Stephen turned from Mulligan and crouched above the ground. He ran his hand through the shingling sand. Long before the *Beagle* set off, lumbering notebooks and dishcloths, Aristotle had begun his classifications. A day like this perhaps, beneath Mount Olympus : he saw boar, lynx and wolf. Now a crab crawls across a doctor's skin.

– Kinch, my God, Kinch, help me with this ...

Stephen looked up : Mulligan was at the shore, pulling a whiteblue form from the water. In the reddening morning sun it appeared like a whalefillet, the bloated underside of a deepfeeder. Stephen schlepped musically through the weedwet shells and litter. A head at first, human and sideparted. Arms, like tuberous fins, had been suckered from the flesh. Quickly, in analytical accretion, the naming of parts raced through Stephen's skull : head, arms, heart. Human hairs crosshatched the stomach, the dumb button of the navel, a pouch of dead minnows in a sack of manufactured loincloth. Impossible father of many.

– For God's sake Stephen, help me pull him out ...

Stephen attempted to move forwards and vomited violently on the dead man's head. Mulligan recoiled, his hands spooning the white torso, dragging him with pantomime animation from the sea.

– My God, you've surpassed yourself now Stephen! Do you serve no function on this earth? Help me wash him ...

The dead man's face had the bloated nonchalance of a jellyfish. His eyes stared into Stephen's eyes, a ruse of cognition : his own double, drained of solutions. As if he had been spewed from the whale of Bray Head, a coughed phlegmball matted with spittle.

– Help me to wash him Dedalus, then take him to shore. He weighs a tonne. We can't let him drift back out …

The man continued to stare, his face the face of his dead mother. Her girlish parted hair, limp and lifeless, blew skywards from his head.

– Move Dedalus, my God, help me …

Stephen took a step forwards and then knelt in the sand, facing Mulligan and the man. Mulligan's hands slipped greasily down the torso of the man then recovered his grip. Stephen, on his knees, propped both of his hands over the top of the ashplant, head bowed, and began to pray :

Liliata rutilantium.
Turma circumdet.
Iubilantium te virginum

When Stephen looked up there was a choir of men helping Mulligan with the body, dragging him slumpways through the sand. Mother, mother. Forsaken. Forgive your son. The man was no longer being pulled by Manannán. Encompassed by radiant confessors : his spirit now lilting with Virgins. Mulligan wants to faux-father my movements. Am I no longer Hamlet to Horatio? Today he makes a Laertes of me. Gertrude sees all : if I play my rôle she will disappear. Must I seek my noble father in the dark rooms of Dublin?

Stephen quicklyrose and walked towards Glasthule. Where am I going? School. I have to be there. Would Deasy accept the dead body as evidence? No. There is not enough of the Eucharist in it. Mulligan, now, would be the saviour of a man ten days dead. He would be hailed for saving that which was lost. And me? A coward. My mind asked me to act and my stomach recoiled. The Englishman would sneer, spooning cream into his tea at breakfast.

Stephen looked back : a party of men in swimwear circled the dead man, now slumped back against the base of the tower. Three gulls wheeled. A crow looked down on them. Stamped its feet and crawed. The sky spoke earthly thunder. Do I see my mother in my mind's eye? The needle she hemmed my blazer with : the stress patterns of the stitches make the music of who I have become.

Stephen walked forwards, stepping between the spouting flames of the crying clams. He looked back to the tower : the figure of a man his own age, dressed in black, paced along the bricked ramparts as an older man clung close to his shoulder. Haines and the milkwoman? No, the older figure was that of a man.

The figure in black pointed up at the clouds.

*Act 1, Scene 3: A room in Polonius' House /
Boys' School in Dalkey. 10am*

– I see – or smell rather – that you've successfully dispensed your wages for liquid.

Mr Deasy pursed his lips, expectant, as Stephen blushed, burst ventricles purpling his cheeks. Stephen spoke :

– A cause for occasion : money and freedom.
– Ah, but that will all end. Real discipline is shaking off your addictions before you have to.
– Shakespeare uncoiled from the earth after late-night drinking with Jonson. Chatterton coiled in his Hoxton sheets after hemlock.
– Their work was done. Yours is still yet to be.
– The necessaries have been embarked upon.
– Then make haste, make haste. Though please leave your creative work for outside of school hours and your drinking for the weekend. Teaching is more akin to the Sciences than the Arts.

Mulligan's words from yesterday echoed : in ten years he'll write something.

The bell rang.

– Class Stephen. And perhaps you might want to stay focussed on what we might call your secular concerns at this school. Ghost stories and riddles are fine for extra-curricular if you'd like to stay after hours unpaid?
– No. I'll keep my curriculum within the contracted hours, Sir.
– Good good. And did you, by any chance, deliver the letter I handed to you?
– Yes Sir, Crawford took it. It will be printed.
– Thank you Stephen. Then we'll say no more about this morning. Let the day begin.

Stephen walked towards class. Youth to itself rebels. What was his curriculum? It had never been defined. Deasy had asked for history and literature. The riddle had been an accident. There was a new class today, older children. Further drowned faces peering from the portholes of poverty. Shakespeare was their birthright : gold lustre for their satchels.

Shy and unbidden, the first child walked into class. Stephen looked up :

– Hullo Sir. Are you Mr Dedalus?
– That has been my downfall.

The boy laughed :

– Armstrong said you would make us laugh.

– If it's a clown you would like I have just seen one at Sandycove.
– A clown on Sandycove Bay, Sir?
– Yes, he was sleeping. He had quite a crowd around him.

More children were gathering in the door. Stephen stood. They took their seats, curiosity curtailing their restlessness. The scraping of chairs settled into the silence of lamb's wool and starched cotton. Stephen addressed them :

– Today we're going to talk about the naming of things.

The boys stared at him, expectant. He continued :

– How is it that everything in the world comes to have a name?

A pink hand rose from the sea of grey faces.

– Yes?
– That's not true, Sir.
– Go on.
– My mother is having another baby and she doesn't know what she'll call it.

The class ruptured in laughter.

Stephen moved sideways in his seat. The bile rose in his stomach : he pressed his hands down on the desk. When they'd visited his father's *alma mater* the word *foetus*, he recalled, was etched into the desk : resilient word defying the years. The jeers settled into silent taunts : ripples of insurrection spread through the class. He had to speak. He swallowed, paused and addressed the landscape of heads : a field of bleached marrows :

– Your name?
– Daniels, Sir.
– Your mother's child : its name will exist in what we call a *subfamily* of naming. What do we know already of this, thing, to be born?

A hand rose.

– It's Irish, Sir?

More jeers. Stephen reflexed : the bile in his stomach recoiled from the laughter.

– What is growing in your mother's stomach is a human. What kind of human?
– A child, Sir?
– Correct. What else will we know on its birth?
– Whether it is a boy or a girl, Sir.
– Excellent. As you can see, there are many levels to which we might name and define. This is what we call *granularity* : the one thing, or form, of the child is defined in small stages. What is at first under-

stood in a general sense comes to be defined through detail. The actual name of the child, its christened name, is just one small detail in how it will become known on earth.

A moth hawked towards Stephen's mouth : he blew it back. Like Aristotle to Pella I am pulled to teach. Is this my Alexander? His palace of mosaics is my field of stones. A Greek leader in each of us.

– The species, then, is a *human*. We then have the *sub-species* : Irish boy called, say, Pogue Mahone.

The class laughed. Stephen looked at Daniels : his face blushed with silent confusion. Too far. Stephen added a caveat to the boy's future sibling :

– The child might then go on to be defined by the wonderful things he goes on to do : poet, say.

A hesitant bashful smile brushed the mouth of Daniels. The moth circled again at Stephen's head : his reflexed hand struck a hindwing. It fell tumbling into the inkwell on his desk. Another hand rose :

– Yes.
– Sir, where did Jesus's body go after he died?

Stephen coughed. He threw the question flying to the class :

– Can anyone answer this?

Three hands rose. Me, Sir, me, me Sir. Stephen scanned the eager faces. And when does optimism end? Life is not a bridge : like yesterday's pier, it disappoints. A boy with freckles across his nose, a map of sunned hours, caught Stephen's attention :

– Yes, you.
– God hid it Sir, so the Romans couldn't find it.

Laughter : mockery pocked with spittle. How long must they live by the blade of insult? Clive Kempthorpe's ragging will be theirs too. Two decades and then done with it.
Must pull them in. Just like young bulls when one runs the others follow.

– I want you now to spend some time making a list of the things that define who you are as individuals : gender, name, hair colour, interests, skills. There are fifty thousand children in Dublin. What are the things that make you unique? You have ten minutes.

To Stephen's surprise the heads bowed as if under highwind : the sound of concentration filled the room. His stomach tried to rupture itself with rude red tongues. He moved crabways to the door and, without excuse, surreptitiously withdrew. He paced to the dusty hut of the staff jakes. Inside, the tang of urine-drenched stone crept cleanly to his senses. He closed the cubicle door behind him, riding the clamping reflexes of his guts. Seaflesh. The greenbile of his mother's bowl. The spatter of unnamed constellations. The class will have their place fixed in the world. I, their teacher, am lost. A woodlouse rowed its logboat out of sight as he spewed. The last ejectemata of his guts landed on its ribbed outhouse. Stephen watched as it tried to swim in the saltgreen outfall of his stomach.

Someone moved in the doorway behind him, a shadow long accustomed to its climate. Deasy. He looked at Stephen with a mix of contempt and mirth : the easeful mien of the self-exiled English.

DEASY: Be thou familiar but by no means vulgar.
STEPHEN: Polonius?
DEASY: Those friends thou hast, and their adoption tried,
    Grapple them to thy soul with hoops of steel.
STEPHEN: Mulligan you mean?
DEASY: Beware of entrance to a quarrel, but being in,
    Bear't that the opposed may beware of thee.
STEPHEN: I held good truck with the Quaker librarian yesterday, it didn't win me an invite to the evening gathering.
DEASY: Neither a borrower nor a lender be; For loan oft loses both itself and friend.
STEPHEN: I fear Mulligan is lost to me despite the alemoney he owes me. I misspent my loan from A.E.
DEASY: This above all : to thine ownself be true.
SEDULOUS: The notion of both truth and ownership of self are both a fallacy. A man in love or under

pressure will reinvent himself for a reprieve. I am
suffering from both states.
SNEEZY: Farewell : my blessing season this in thee!

Stephen wiped the sick from the seat as Deasy watched, then sneezed.

Easygreasysneezydeasy Stephen thought, wiping his mouth on his sleeve.

PROTEUS

*Act 1, Scene 4 : The Platform /
mudflats of Sandymount Strand. 11am*

Stephen looked back at his tower. Hölderlin. If I stay will I go mad? Those two would drive me to it. Like a bad joke : an Englishman, an Irishman and a poet walk into a pub.

A blackheaded gull dipped its hooded head, the cowl of a crook, into the static stream of seawater. It bobbed nonchalantly in the cool water. On a bench overlooking the bay a tiny brown pair of toddler's shoes had been left, toetips down, waiting for their owner.

Wet wood broke in limp strips and stuck to his shoes. O Mary Rose, my heart. Yesterday I held gold now wood is my steerage. The doctor and Englishman left me amongst the swine. Under gaslights and stars. Drunk my estate and left me for broke. Barabbas in cahoots with Shylock. Leonard the martyr. Now I have a dead man to contend with. His eyes the eyes of my mother. Full fathom five my mother lies.

A man lifted a brick and hurled it for his dog to fetch. The dog watched it dunk : turned back to face its owner. The man pitched another : the dog plunged, marking the watertide on its legs. Then waited. On the third throw the dog followed, swam earsback to the circling plod of the stone : its grim snout fixed as a pig's. Its leans ribs slick against the incoming tide. It swam to shore and howled gruffly at its owner. Stephen watched passively as the stones clashed with the Doppler arrows of the tide.

Who was the man in black I saw on the ramparts earlier? Haines? Refusing to contribute to the milk he slakes each morning. Will Mulligan still want to drain his draught of Rhenish with me? Mulligan says he will Hellenise me. Am I a false poet to have Greek taught to me by a doctor? He speaks in iambic pentameter : behind his steelblade there is a gift. We prick each other like warring schoolboys. He tries to conquer me with Shakespearian rhythms : the Sassensach wants his morning rashers he said. That was yesterday, today food is beyond me. Still need those slips from the library counter. Must find water. Tongue clefts the hoof of my palate. Cartesian aftershock of liquor. These Dublin gulls choir in unison. The influence of the revivalists : Yeats will have them at the Abbey. There is no scope for a soloist.

Before he'd moved to Paris his mother would scrub his ears, lather his neck : readying him for lectures. Was a lethargy in him then? At the time he had thought she had enjoyed it most but no : it was him. Softsuds scoring his extremities. The hands that had attached him to her paps, weaned him to solids, were also the hands that cleansed him for school. A poor case, she had said. Could I have not prayed? No, my prayer was in the song. Who will go drive with Fergus now? I am through with lyric.

Overthought had brought him to this : the lull of sirenmusic. Metrics in stanzaforms. My muse and music hit the rocks : the rocks are my mother. I will see my mother's face rise beneath another's lashes. Each glance leaves a scoremark. Goldveined platitudes are in the past : my epic will take me with it or else bring the world crashing. I will poke out the solipsistic I of Yeats.

Stephen looked up from the shore towards the city : a city mapped with the names of his writers. Newman at North Strand Road, Ibsen at Talbot Place. Now Swinburne at Sandycove. Would his own words, the words he wrote, call him back in echoed whispers after he'd ceased? Writing for the surcease of sensation. At university his conscience had become a monster that had begat unrest in another student's mind. Every so often he would need to speak : confession without the collar. Mulligan was now listener and axeman. God, he would be crucified for that incident on the beach. I cannot go back. I have lined my nest with the acids of my innards. Mulligan would send his secret back to the English. Inform against his bloodline. Ach, I do not believe this : in the vortex of aesthetics, ethics and women's elastics I am tangled. The thorns are on the inside. The plump upstart would sell him back to the seat of Elizabeth and his secondbest language. Hoopsa, hoopsa.

Bacterial absinthe contracted in his stomach. A rockpool of crabs and crustaceans. Should have eaten. Took the bun from Leonard in the cabman's shelter. Why did he show me the photograph of his wife? Dame Partlet, the hen. Mistress Quickly. It was too late for me to act. Glass smashed, sinning done. Would I though? Through the fortress of the Jesuits touch another man's wife? The heave of her breasts. Desire forked hot in Stephen's cheeks. His trailing leg attached to a doily of seaweed.

ENTER GHOST.

Across the beach the figure of a woman in white hovered. Who will drive with Fergus now? O mother, my heart. The figure dispersed and reappeared thirty feet along the cove.

GHOST BECKONS *DEDALUS*.

In awkward agile strides Stephen crossed the beach away from the opaque outline of his mother. The National Library, will I go? Deasy's words wound through his mind and anchored : *yours is still yet to be*. First the doctor and now the teacher : all seemed to know the ferment of his work. As if the yeast of his gifts had been pinched from their snuffbox. On other shores he would distil his green to gold. The hoofirons of his rhythms would canter in iambs and trochees. The final molossus would take ten years.

Stephen stopped at the rustcockled railings. A woman in white stood before him. Not his mother : younger, her lacewhite skin shone in the lumens of the seafront. He stood back as she passed. Her eyes looked into him : deep ambers. He willed her to pass : she did not.

– You're Stephen Dedalus.
– That is the sin of my father.

She looked at him, smiling.

– You're a poet, I've read your words.
– That is something I can't apologise for.

Stephen, conscious of his scent and the fagstumps of his teeth, willed himself to move towards Strand Road. She spoke :

– Have you read the poetry of Yeats?

He stopped.

– Yes. And sang it.
– Do you think he's good?
– I do not know what I should think. His metrics conform. How did you know who I am? I don't recognise your face. I don't think we've met.

Stephen blushed at the lone word *face* : her awareness that he'd noticed her beauty. The cloudless climes of her features.

– I live at Glasnevin. Sometimes I weave pages for the women of the Dun Emer Industries. I am studying and will then do what Ireland expects of its women. I saw your name in the university journal. I liked your poem.
– That poem was weak and is distant to me now. I am trapped in new experiences I am yet to find words for.

A jackdaw rattled its syrinx in the bush behind her. He rubbed his eyes : the tang of Monto was on his fingers. He made to move past her, up towards the road. She did not speak.

As he walked he felt the weight of her : she followed without moving. Her eyes the weight of fathoms in the back of his head. Seaweed blacker than oilslicks withered to a skeletal bracken. Stephen stopped to pick it, rootless seaflower, from the sand. A mass of grains lent it weight then fell away one by one : Thermopylae's spent. Each thing now is hers. This weed no longer weed, that gull an archangel : omens and portents. Has my mother taken her form, taken her body to give issue to her rage? The girl, my mother, will suck my unpraying soul and spit it in a clambucket. No, she is pure. Her eyes. Books. Poetry. She knows the Me I want too. Am I dreaming?

The sand took on a slimegreen tinge. He followed the exaggerated *U*s of hoofprints through the sand. The surface blitzed with the pockmarks of worms which had coalesced to sleep in bundles of tired *S* shapes. O shadowdance, my heart. Is she here to stay?

In the distance a dog ran helterskelter across the sand, its cantering form without centre : a creature with twoheads. I have seen the day's corpse. Dog yesterday, today man. Tomorrow? The exorcised viscera of the Roman Catholic Apostolic Church.

I did not kill that man. Ten days dead he was. My God, his cheeks like saturated shellfish. His eyes : searching. My mother's eyes. Her hair growing from his pate. Stephen crouched in the sand and sobbed into his hands. The tears had the scent of old alcohol and dried sweat.

His ashplant collapsed in the sand beside him. The dog came and sniffed his weltering grief, tailwagging, no titbits here, and ran wetmouthed back to its owner. Goodboy, goodboy.

Stephen dried the fretmarks of his grieving. Beside him the red and white tibula of a razorclam lay flat in the sand. He lifted it, emptied of flesh. Like a pipe he took it to his lips and blew : a high constant chord flew from the instrument. A sound that is. Like the Abbey revivalists it plays constant to nature. He smashed the frail shell on a stone : its longwhite form shattered into a mosaic of shinclean pieces.

Stephen stood to walk. He picked his ashplant and made three steps; his left heel slipped in the sand. He kept upright and looked : jellyfish. Ventricles flamed in orangered, betraying their transparency. At the flat centre of its structure the intricate pattern of his boot had left an imprint. By chance we passed : two crops of Ireland knitted to one form. Will I go to the city? Yes, the library slips. He walked towards the station. A jackdaw peered from the black slatless gap in a cottage roof. He turned on to Guilford Road, alongside walls knitted with the same sandstone as the tower. A dunnock dipped into a hedge : its minsicule heart exploding in fistulas of song.

Before, many years before, on the beach, no words had passed between him and the girl with the rolled-up skirt. Their souls had conversed. His soul was singing with the same profanity now, only words had knitted them together. Their hearts confessed it : *docome, docome.*

Did he need a woman, this woman, in order to write? A witness to the cost, a voyeur of the limited hours of creation? She called to him from the coast he was yet to persuade her to leave.

I will write here. Must find those library slips. Am I right to swear it true? Hamlet thought so : *Now to my word*. Wild and whirling words. Will she help me find form?

Who can I speak to of this? The candied tongue licks absurd pomp. Malachi is not Horatio : though he does laugh at reason. The balance is awry.

Dust in white plumes exploded around the shreds of his shoes. His heart pumped the weak barrel of his chest. Who was she? A binder of Yeats. Tied to the backways of Celtic singsong. Her eyes : flints of darkcoves. Youth in his mother's white. What could it mean? I have not yet broken bread and already I have vomited on a deadman and overseen the ascension and ghost of my mother. And tomorrow?

I must make the station. What are these winding roads for? Dublin's nose blossoms on the city's imports. Front yard and back. Decoys from reality : there, a flamingo in ceramics. Copy of a copy, void of the artist's makebelieve.

Behind, from an opened window laden with books, a teenage boy shouted at Stephen. *Oy, Oy!* My ownself, peeling its tonguebells from past days. What *did* she want from me, or I from her? Her confidence, bosom : permission to write. If she comes, comes with me, the words will come too. Her scent of rosewood. Foam replaces ash.

He looked up at a house that seemed to be made for Gretel : an inlaid stone read *1894*. Newbuild for old lovers. Its gutter ringed with red icing. No, take it with you beyond the shores. Am I now in love? Was she the insubstantial image I've looked for? Image made flesh : both : to ideate and hold. It had happened as he thought : in a secret place. Weakness and nervousness stuck to him. He had stood his ground. Then walked from it. The ache of his head punctuated with the thumping stress of each heartbeat :

Dedalus, Dedalus, Dedalus.

MAPS : PART I

*Elsinore. A platform before the castle /
the Martello Tower*   35

*A room of state in the castle /
the Forty Foot*   36

*A room in Polonius' House /
Boys' School in Dalkey*   37

*The Platform /
mudflats of Sandymount Strand*   38

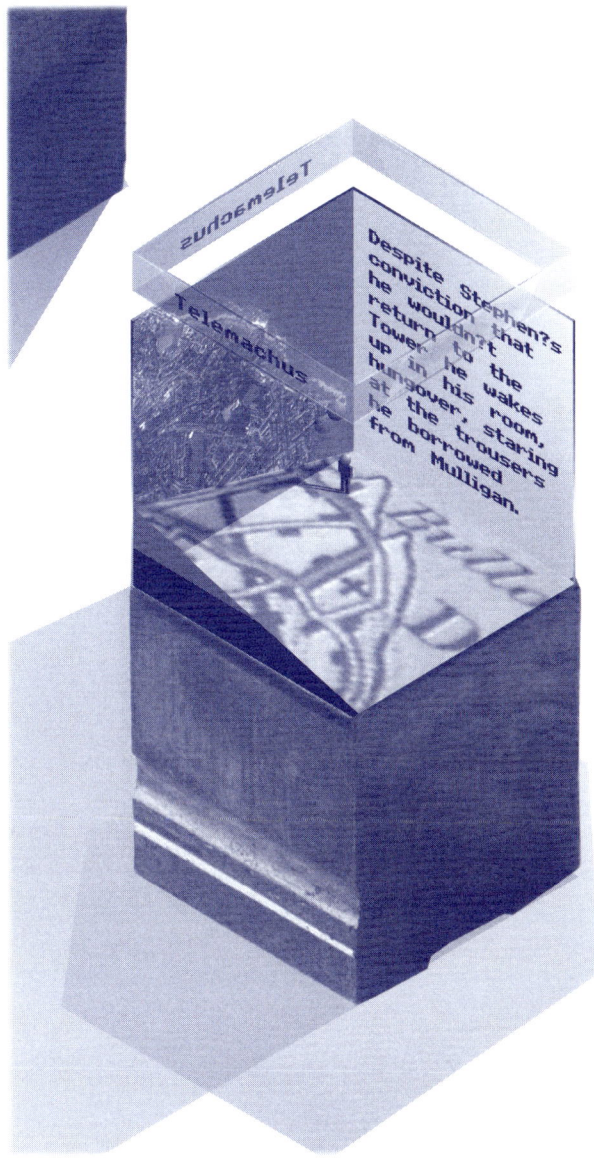

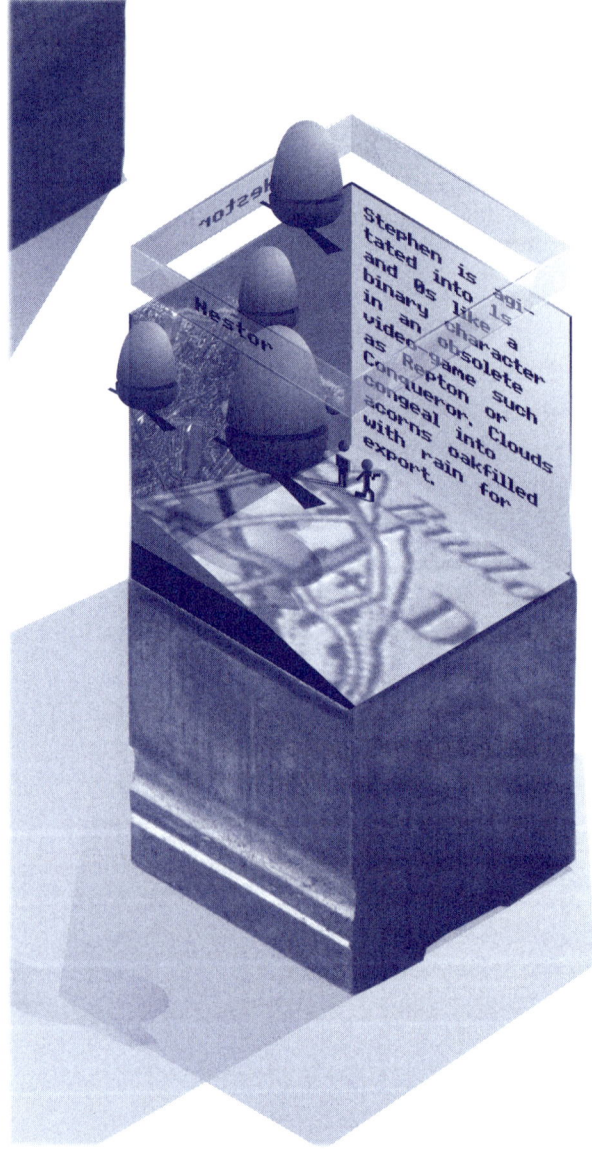

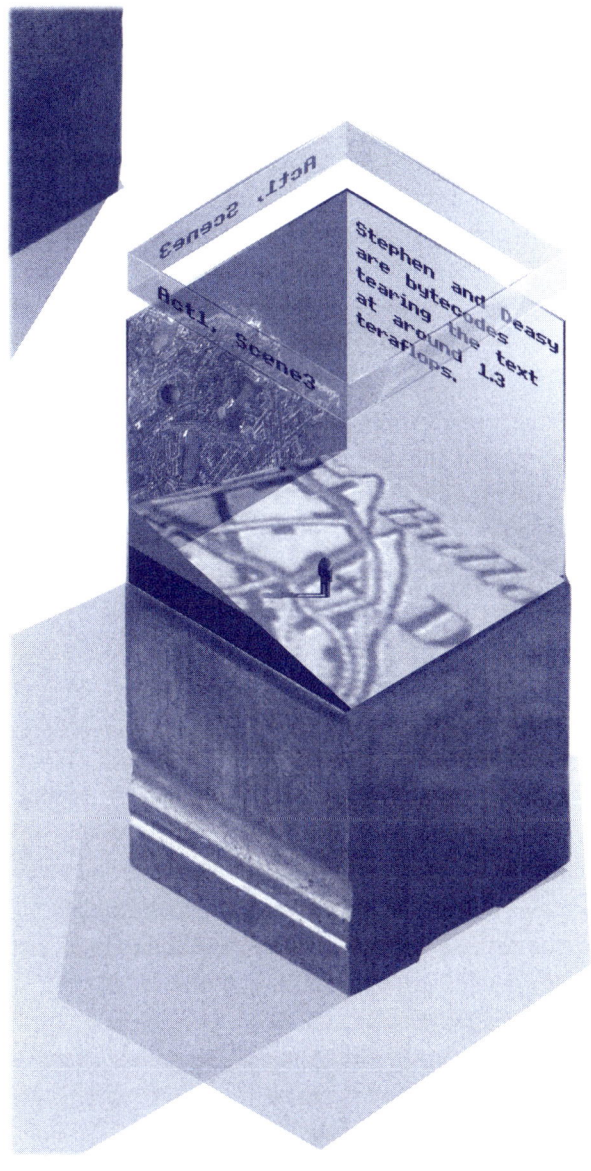

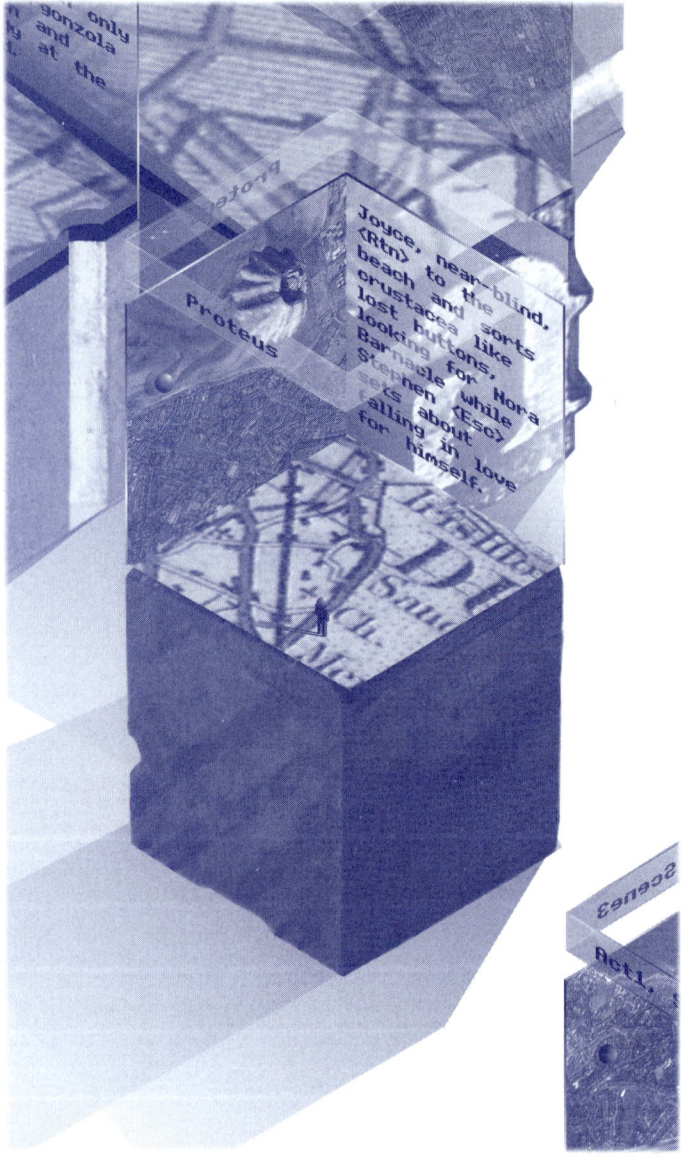

Part II

CALYPSO

Act 1, Scene 5: Another part of the platform /
7 Eccles Street. 8am

Cautious tired Leopold Bloom picked up a piece of paper from the kitchen table. The long loops of Stephen's handwriting rose and fell in sharp points. The same as the language exercises he'd shown me. Different this is, a poem.

Bloom read out loud the writing of Stephen Dedalus. The cat listened : its eager ears listening for the pussenswords.

Across the solitary space of thought
Across the roar of planet's tomb
I mouth, forget, this life you brought
Breathe these words to your hollow womb

The melody of poetry, nothing else like it. Song of course, though that moves forwards without you. Poetry you can stop : read again.

Still doubled, he re-read the poem, this time in silence.

Across the solitary space of thought
Across the roar of planet's tomb
I mouth, forget, this life you brought
Breathe these words to your hollow womb

Death of a mother : such a loss. So young too. Only happens once of course. Strange how I thought of her last night, in Monto, first time in years. Not like that with Papli of course : can barely shake him off long enough to smell the flowers. If thou didst ever thy dear father love. Dignam's funeral must have done it, scattering all that dust. I wonder if it would be the same if I hadn't seen him after? His face already changed. Hairs sprouting the nostrils. Wonder if things get hairier before the skeletal stage? What is it they're called? *Lycanthropes*. Doomed for a certain hairs to walk the night. Check the dental records after : this beast seems to be your father. Could ask Kelleher I suppose.

The cat rubbed in arched hunger around Bloom's legs.

– Poorpussenscan'tsurviveonpoemsnoshecan'tcanshe…

Bloom carefully placed two slices of toast onto the tray and added a small pot of steaming tea. In a rhapsody of concentration he walked up the stairs, clattering the bedroom door with the wooden tray. Molly raised her nightwarm frame from the duvet, yawning.

– How did you sleep?
– Mmhhm … o.k. …

– Here's tea, and toast.
– Did you get my lotion?
– I'll go back today. Time got the better of me, between the funeral and the hospital. You've heard about Mrs Purefoy?
– No.
– Boy. Hearty and well. Quite a gathering at Holles Street.
– Surprised you could withstand going there.
– Wanted to be there, raise a toast. I was out late, sorry if I …
– You told me when you got back. Half-asleep you were.
– Did I? Quite worn out, the funeral, I think, did it. Quite exhausting.
– Why was he here?
– Who?
– The poet.
– I brought him back. Quite lost he is, since his mother's death you know.
– That was more than a year ago.
– He needs some help. A steer. His path has wavered, the wrong friends, drink …
– And you want to help him?
– Yes. I. I thought he might help us too. A tour you know, perhaps of Britain … his voice is quite exceptional, runs in the family, from his father's side.

A small envelope of toast halted in Molly's hand : her eyes crossed Bloom's eyes.

– Well you know quite well that things are fixed with Boylan, plans can't be changed willynilly like that. I have my career.
– That I understand, but perhaps your gift is being undersold?
– He's – ambitious for me. We travel on Monday.

She folded the quadrant of stiff bread into her mouth and chewed hastily. That bread without poppyseeds. His hand patted and flattened the fleshtousled sheets. In the oval dressingtable mirror the right side of his face reflected back the slumped form of another man.

He coughed before speaking, his eyes side-on to hers. In hastening selfsurprise he spoke as if the words of another :

– When he writes to you he should address you as my wife.
– He addresses me as an artist and that is how he knows me. I'm not to be attached to a man who is hardly *attached* to any other thing ...

Through the opening of the door the wellfed cat proudly entered. Husband and wife looked. A delicate music paused in cadences against the window : rain.

– I am attached, Bloom said, to my wife and daughter.
– *Phtuh*, and what about that little bitch you're writing to?

Bloom bristled. His words hedged then nested in his throat. The cat taptapped its paws on his trousers.

– I. I put an advert out for an assistant.
– *Hu*. To assist you with what?
– You're aware that I've long wanted to write, I thought this summer I would at last make a start.
– Well, I would have thought that you might have written something first that might need assisting with. That would be like me arranging a tour with no repertoire. And your assistant had to be a woman did she?
– That is a convention. I would need someone to type for me, the women's colleges you see.
– Could you have not told me about your plans?
– I, planned to.
– And, well, tell me, what is a wife supposed to do when her husband is sending letters to some other … woman … on the other side of Dublin?
– I only wrote out of loneliness.
– Loneliness! And what time did you come to bed last night? Don't talk to me about loneliness!
– For too long now our relations have been strange to me, and unnatural.

Bloom ran his hand along the sleek arch of the cat. His spirits lifted : did she resent his letter to Martha because of the feelings she still had for him? Perhaps his British Isles tour idea would work out … She would agree to it, perhaps, if he stopped writing to Martha? Bloom smelled the fresh hope of negotiation. He coughed. Should he say that he knew about Boylan, an exchange for her frankness about his letter from Martha? As he thought the silence spread its wings; outside a bird clattered a gutter. The creaking wardrobe spoke, reinforcing the silence, as if some posturing writer had been incarcerated inside and was running low on air.

A soft thud and clatter rose up the staircase : post. He pictured another letter from Martha falling on the mat. No, she wouldn't write to him here, she'd send it to the Post Office. He'd taken care of that. The fire of his words dissolved in a milky eucharist on his tongue. Molly spoke :

– Will you collect that, or shall I? It could be another letter from Milly.

Bloom rose, the withheld words singed like moths in the air around him. He looked down the stairs : a paper-white flag lay on the mat.

TO / MISS MARION BLOOM

Boylan's hand. The same hand as. No. Mustn't. Business. Must let her make up her own mind. Bloom shouted heartily up the silent staircase :

– There's post on the side for you. I'm going out for a while.

Bloom closed the door behind him, its unsnipped frame cushioned by an invisible pillow of air. Distracted, sparrows and tits tweeted from the turrets of the chimneys :

Tu Bloo, Tu Bloo –

Bloom felt his heart as he walked. Funny how words spoken sound different than inside. Feel like a ghost watching, trying to explain her actions. Adulterous beast, can't pretend I don't. Wonder what if she'll? No. Headstrong. No mother as a girl, makes her own decisions. Can't be dissuaded. Though something of feeling for me still, hope in her wrath over the Martha letter. She knows my secret too. An equal swap? Dangerous game for us, stones in a glass house. Will we watch each other? Not much to see here. Bloom felt into the leather headstrap of his hat and pulled out the paper : HENRY FLOWER.

Milly, phoo, phoo, Tu Bloo –

Can go down the river, like *Elijah*. List, list, O list! Bloom struck a black line through the name : ~~HENRY FLOWER~~. Must not let my bed be a couch for adultery. There, new morning. Feels different written. Fight fire with fire. The serpent that stung me now wears my crown.

Molly, phoo, phoo, Tu Bloo!

Come, bird, come : Bloom looked up : Simon Dedalus and Martin Cunningham were walking along the street towards him. The staggering Dedalus held upright in the arms of the righteous Cunningham.

– Okay, Bloom? I'm just helping Simon home …
– Ah, yes, I see.

Simon spoke, the words eliding sidewise from his mouth like wet figs sliding from a nutcracker :

– Ah, Bloo … Dublin's bravest … or stu … Doom'd for a certain term … Where's your wife?
– She's … Why do you?
– Come now Simon, let's get you home.

Cunningham pulled at Simon's arm, his legs asp-like, twisted and rooted where they were. Never a drunk in all of Dublin but he's a waste of voice. Bloom spoke :

– Will you be okay Martin, I have business that I …
– Yes, we'll soon be back, Simon now …
– I'm sorry that my words o … offend you … I have business too, one more for the road Martin …
– There's no offence to me, said Bloom.
– None to you?
– I was thinking of the offence to your son.
– By the balls of St Patrick, don't try to guess what's between us … listen …

He called Bloom towards him.

– Promise me one thing?

– What is it?
– Don't let him know you saw me ... You too Martin ...
– We will not.
– Swear it then?
– I swear, now ...
– You too Bloo ...
– Yes, I swear, but I really think you should let Martin take you home.
– Here, swear it on this.

Simon Dedalus pulled from his stained blazer a miniature St John's Gospel : cowled thumbprints muddied its pages. Martin spoke :

– Simon, we have sworn already.
– On the Gospel, swear't!

The drunken asp flowered itself in the scent of nightfumes :

– Swear you won't tell him you've seen me!

THEY SWEAR.

– Hic. Hic. Hic et. Ubique. Hic. Flacking hiccoughs!

He wiped his mouth.

– Come, right gentlemen ... well, we know, we could ... wonderful day, hotter than a horny wink in the

Monto ... sorry, if we listen we speak ... and ...and there we can be if we would ... the curse of the son that I was born to try and put him right ... let us go Martin.

The men walked away from Bloom, revenants heading back to the catacombs. Strange, thought Bloom, how a drunk suddenly sobers when he needs a last drink.

EXEUNT BLOOM.

```
You are on a residential street, facing SE.
>GOTO 51

You are on a platform before a castle.
>GOTO 152
```

LOTUS EATERS

Act 2, Scene 1: A room in Polonius' house / Eccles Street, through Dublin to Sir John Rogerson's Quay. 10am

I wonder why Martha wants to know Molly's scent? Strange female impulse, be the woman you hate. Smell what another's skin is like. Be seen as you imagine. Not sure I'll write. Now that Molly knows. How could she? Must have seen me writing in the kitchen. Smelt something strange about me. Will have it out with her again later. Will I? What would the court of law defence say : driven to lewd acts by the actions of an unfaithful wife? Difference between touch and fantasy. Was my letter more than fantasy? Phew. Pen mightier than the sword. A *word* in sword, never seen that before. The pen is mightier than the word. No, makes no sense. The gun is mightier than the sword. Did I want Molly to catch me so I can have it out with her? Bring it to a head. No, not sure I. Gameplay. Double bluff. Could I have someone keep a watch on her? Make inquiries of her behaviour. No, know enough already. Was just about to think something, about to think. Something. I. That girl again. Not in me today, she looks different too. Funeral perhaps? Tidy little piece she seemed in Dlugacz's yesterday. Wouldn't mind a cut of that. Whack. And those hips. Wonder what it feels like, moving knowing you're being watched. Get all your groceries in one go with a woman like that. Enough trouble at home, will have to watch what I watch. Hard not to. The little cripple girl on the beach too, turned her into a Venus. See what you think. Let the mind fill in the gaps. Molly's flame elsewhere. Funny how his name. No. Don't judge a book by its cover. Judge a cover by its cover. Must write that. Look, she's gone. Fine hams too. Though not a patch on Molly.

What would I have found if I'd have went home early yesterday? Mr Bloom I saw them leaving together. He entered with a bag of ripe groceries. Bang on time he was. I called you naughty boy because I do not like that other world. Pick up Molly's potion then go to the cemetery, ask them to check my name in the book. Shame they left my name out from the paper, wouldn't want anyone to look back and think I wasn't there. Donation too. Generous in its way. Not that it counts in the face of such a loss. Tuppence to the Gods. Who's that? Can't be. God. What are the … too late. Duck in here.

Blushing Bloom stepped into the doorway of the bustling café. Plates clanked in competition with clattering teaspoons : a drunken circus of ceramics. Too late, Bridie Kelley spoke :

– I was surprised to see you last night … it has been a number of years …
– I … I was looking out for my young friend.
– It was kind of you to pick him up like that, after his friends had left.

– It was the least I could do. He's, having a difficult time.
– I see him there often. He's known to us.

Bloom looked more closely at her face : sleeplessness had bore deep grooves into her skin. Twenty years before, I. First time. My first, not hers. Could I have saved her?

– I saw you from a distance; I'd taken the absinthe ... I saw your friend, his trousers stained, his face pale as his shirt, he looked sick ... like a ghost ...
– His drinking makes him unwell.
– Or love. He looks like a man sick for love.
– Did he tell you of this?
– He mentioned Paris, it was hard to ... follow ... he held my arm, his eyes distant, then he let me go.
– I am sorry for this. He lost his mother you see, tragic loss.
– I will speak to the matron, ask the women to spare him. For his own good!
– Yes, his habits must be changed. I'm trying to involve him in a project, a creative endeavour.
– You are as kind as you were. Remember you gave me more money than you had to, that time?
– I'm sorry, I ...
– You are a kind man, perhaps I might say ... quite feminine in your way ...
– Do you mean to say, about that time?
– Not that no, I mean ... you're different than other Dublin men ...

The door of the café swung on a rusted hinge and a man, wiping his mouth with a sleeve, walked between them. Bloom made to leave :

– I must go, my wife, you see …
– Could you give me some money? It's not been easy, not since …
– Take this, please. Don't let anyone see.

Bloom took coins from his pocket and discreetly placed them in her hand. After she'd left the scent of far-off spices lingered, soft as rainwater in the doorway.
Bloom looked. Left. Right. Safe. He walked four doors and entered under the tiled white sign of SWENY'S, the bell clanging behind him. Soaps, like matured cheese, sat squat in the window. Phials for Virol sat in size order : dolls without heads. AN IDEAL FAT FOOD FOR CHILDREN AND INVALIDS. Future of food, I wonder, all in a teaspoon. Four times a day, four seconds to eat. Still, good extra nourishment. If Rudy. No. God's way she said.
The shelves looked down, sentries of glass apothecary jars : green, blue, red. Lifts the mood. Especially with the scent. Bloom walked back to the desk and trilled down on the bronzeplated button besides the COMPOUNDING DEPARTMENT. In the glass cabinet in front of him rows of blue and red pocketsized packets were available for purchase : FINEST TASTELESS CASTOR OIL and LINIMENT OF IODINE POISON (for external use only). Wonder what would happen if I swallowed? No, put it in his Guinness. Hoo. Does he drink Guinness? Milder on the throat. Two packets please doctor.

– I have an order to collect, for Molly Bloom.

The pharmacist turned the name over in his mouth, spitting the soft plosive in concentrated syllables : *Bloom. Bloom. Bloom.* More masculine than Flower, though can mean the same. Don't know why I called myself ...

– This seems to be the one. 7 Eccles Street. Should have been collected yesterday. Did you bring the bottle?
– Yes, I was out until late. Sidetracked. Dignam's funeral. I have the bottle.

Bloom handed the bottle across the counter to the chemist : with well-practised efficiency the man took it in his hand and turned his back on the customer. Hammam again? No, quite worn out. Might put me to sleep, slide under the suds. Drown facedown. Flounder like a fish out of water.

– Quite an unusual potion this. Orange, benzoin, almond. Your good lady having trouble sleeping?
– Er, yes. Quite. How much?
– This won't keep her up.

Bloom blushed.

– The cost?
– Twelve pence, with the soap from yesterday.

Bloom's smooth hand reached into his pocket and keyed the tune of loose coins. Must ask for a few weeks longer for the ad. Income trickles into streams this time of year, good thing to press the tourists. He placed the coins one by one on the rosewood counter. Ten. Eleven. Twelve. There. Wonder if I enjoy? No. Pinch on the wrist. I said I'm a sadist said de Sade. Hoo. De Sade said I'm a sadist I said. Wait. I'm sad I'm a sadist said de Sade. Must write it down. Right what I said to Molly too, make a start on that writing this summer.

Bloom stopped at the newstand and, tipping his hat to the seller, exchanged a coin for the *Dublin Evening Mail*. He read as he walked.

Liverpool could be worth it. First leg of the tour. Nice humour they have. Whole flocks, like gulls, went over. Steam Packet Company does trips, eight hours by sea passage. *Cheap Excursions : golden memories*. Every Saturday and Sunday I think. Ah, Kipling : written a piece on army reform. 'The Army of a Dream' will appear in *The Morning Poets*.

Curious ad here : *why boil clothes? It weakens fibre, loosens texture, shrinks fabric. There isn't the least necessity of it.* FELS-NAPTHA *stops half the rubbing and all the boiling.* Writer needs to limber up a little, not enough art. Can't tell someone 'there isn't the least necessity of it', why should they believe? More of a game it is. Start with the words, a slight jingle. Sense of something new. Others are doing it, miss out if you don't. As if the world goes on in a dance they're not part of. Then you hook them see, relief they feel that it didn't pass them by. Doesn't matter if they don't want it. By-the-by that is. Make more money by pretending not to care about making it : there's the rub.

Will I write this Summer? Must fix up that desk. Place it downstairs facing St George's. Good light through the garden. Get up an hour earlier than usual, five hundred words before Molly's breakfast. What would that be each week? Five is ten, fifteen double add five : three thousand five hundred words a week. Three months ten thousand. Harvest for Autumn, knuckle down in Winter. Fingerless gloves and a scented candle. Cat curled before the hot coals. A whole world to go into. Would it work like that? No. Headscratching and distractions. Bits and pieces. Molly shouting down the stairs. Milly looking for her needles. House needs dusting. Watch Molly watch me withdraw. Would she pull me back? She has her music. Lose something if I turned to face my words. Worth a try. No, try talk first. See where that gets us. Time for the steelpen later.

ADVERTISEMENT » [x]

SKIN SO DELICATE WHITE LIKE WAX

Online offers on women's skin products, big June discounts:

Neutrogena Pore Refining Daily Cleanser: The alpha and beta hydroxy acids in Neutrogena Pore Refining Daily Cleanser dissolve makeup and grime.
$7.99. <u>BUY NOW</u>.

spreynolds : I started using this about a month ago and it is amazing. It actually does what the description says!

You are trying to fold a NEWSPAPER as you walk,
but the wind is trying to read it.

?Take the tram
>GOTO 59

?Explore a room in the castle
>GOTO page 153

HADES

*Act 2, Scene 2: A room in the castle /
Glasnevin cemetery. 11am*

Rattle my bones. Much nicer on the tram than that carriage yesterday. Threw me quite out of kilter. Rudy. Death makes him a kind of pauper. Gone. Nobody owns him now. Free to grow as he will. No, always a boy of course, no point picturing him like that. Hopeless. Don't know what came over me last night : like a dwarf he was, a small usher, holding that lamb. Wonder if Molly thinks too sometimes? Must. Mother's love. Can it be much different? Of course, that's what she meant when she asked how I could face going to Holles Street. Right in her way : must have left its legacy in Monto. Should I ask her about it, how she feels? Too raw still? If not now, when? Must try face on, talk through it. Grow back together perhaps. Flesh and blood of both parents, more flesh for the mother. Blood too. Like a bloodbath it was, crimson bedspreads. Best not. Wonder though if she? If I asked?

First born just out by a vowel. Milly. Molly. If we had another could carry it on : Mally, Melly, Mully. No, none the same. Plucked the best already : best names for the best girls. My girls? Nice ring to it. Still time. I have a daughter. She is mine. Rhythm and rhyme see : this year I shall write.

No mother of her own of course, brings her back in a way. As if children could make up the wrongs. Trundle in, bringing their own. Us too, thinking we know. Ironing my shirt the day before she was born, pressing down the collars. Paper sailboats, wondering if it was a boy. Pressed seven shirts to last the week. As soon as I saw her I wanted to hold, forgot about the shirt : pink streaks down the sleeves. Curds of milk. Quite the dresser back then I was. A snappy dresser with a new baby.

Good job Dignam took insurance. Leave behind morsels for the children, peck up what they can like sparrows.

Mr Bloom paused to look in detail at a dead mouse curled into a corner of the moving tram. Wonder would it be warm if I touched it? Looks like ink on its back. Printer's devil. Wonder why it came here to die? Bad crumbs I expect. Chemical flour. Quite binding.

From the window of the clattering tram Bloom saw freshshaven Simon Dedalus walk into Mulligan's pub, Poolbeg Street. Awkward that was this morning. Couldn't get out of my way. These drunks turn their own heads into fontanelles. Make out they look after each other. In cahoots. When the bar breaks the baby will fall. That time I saw them walking the wrong way up the tramline. Close to midnight, went for a walk to clear the headache. Don't think they saw. Linking along the tracks. Wonder if some kind of joke? Back before Mrs Dedalus had passed. Death wish then. Perhaps he'll pass through it, drink away the grief. Horses for courses. Throwaway. See the light one day and stay at home the next. Pipe and slippers. Irishman's home is his candle. Castle. Unfortunate slip. Yes but all burns out one way or the other. Wonder if Bridie was right about Stephen, that a woman might save him?

At Glasnevin Mr Bloom descended the tram then turned to the driver :

– Dead mouse back there, under the rear seat to the left.

The driver looked at him, in silence. Bloom continued :

– I just thought you might want to clear it. Disease you know. Especially in this heat.
– If you would like to remove it, please do. I have these passengers to take.

Bloom stood down. Quite the nerve. Never in all my. City changing of course, no one cares enough. A second to clear up, save a life. Should have put it in my handkerchief. Gave it a burial.

Bloom approached the gates of the cemetery. Here. Here we are, back again. Missed me the first time. Best not come a third : a chance too much. Here it was I mentioned John Menton's crushed hat. Seemed put out. Best left perhaps? I would like to know.

In the distance across the mushroom-coloured headstones a tall lean figure moved. His form wavered as the man bent down to touch the earth, then reappeared. Mackintosh. Hanging around Dignam's earth. Soil like tousled sheets. Long sleep. I wonder why he's, maybe I could?

Bloom took the narrow path away from the Parishioner's Office. Curious as to the register. M'intosh was his name. Old friend of Dignam's perhaps? Altar boys from school maybe, bookends. Wonder if they get a hit from the incense? Quite intoxicating I expect. Take a nip from the chalice when the Priest's not looking.

– Hello, I saw you across the way. I'm Mr Bloom.

Curious smiling Leopold Bloom held out his hand. The man looked up at him. There was a twist in his face, as if the Gods had given him a pinch on dispatch. Eyes no more than slits. Weasellike.

– I thought, Bloom said, that you might be a friend of Dignam's?

The man wiped his mouth, spoorcrumbs of soil stuck to his lips.

– Dignam?
– Paddy Dignam, buried yesterday. That's his grave you're standing on.

The man in the mackintosh looked down, his feet wrapped in strips of leather that might once have been shoes.

– This one, or that one?
– This one.

Bloom pointed between the man's feet.

– Heart attack, Bloom said. Quite unexpected.
– I'm helping, the man said, to tend the grounds. My job is to bury the dead, not make friends with them. To pick out this man would be one in ten thousand.
– Ah, quite right, Bloom said. The earth. Soil, needs tending.
– If you don't mind I've got work to do. The headstone will be arriving this afternoon.
– Right, yes. Good day.

As Bloom walked the man shouted after him:

– Have you a daughter?
– I have.
– Let her not walk out here alone, it's not safe.

Bloom followed the path back to the office. Turned to cold : stonewhite he's made me. If the sun breeds maggots in a dead dog. Quite the snub. Fancy looking down his nose with shoes like that! Less than a hobo's. And those eyes, phew! Like pennyslots. Face like a whacked squash. Smelt a bit too. Suppose you would, creeping around here all day. Kind of mildew on his breath. Turn into the dead while still living. Seemed to have forgotten he was still here then resented the pleasantries. Must have woke him from the underworld.

In the adjacent section of the cemetery a kind of canopy had been built in a hollowed-out space between the headstones and a troupe of what looked like travelling actors were gathered around a rope, pulling on it. A brown canvas form emerged from its puckered state on the ground. Summer fête perhaps? Little close to the headstones. Excuse me, trying to sleep here. Just stood on my. Would you mind if you went a hundred yards? Obliged.

Bloom arrived at the Parishioner's Office and stamped both feet twice. He knocked three times.

A small man with white hair opened the door. He was pristinely pressed in black and white raiments. Bloom spoke first :

- I have come to check my name was added correctly to the register for Dignam's funeral.
- I will need to be quick, my daughter is not well today. If you were here would you not know if your name was added correctly?
- I believe I wrote it out right, I seem to remember. The newspaper though you see, it left out an 'l' in 'Bloom'.
- Ah, but that effective defective comes from the press. A misreading perhaps, an error of type?
- Yes, I had considered that, however I did just want to confirm that was the case.
- I will be quick – brevity is the fire of my work – please bear with me.

The man disappeared inside, closing the door behind him. Clean at least, looked fresh from a boiling. Dealing with the ecumenical matters you see, careful not to touch the soil. Soul and soil : hadn't considered. Slip of a vowel upends everything.

The door reopened.

– Your name appears in the book as Mr. L. Bloom. The mistake I believe will be with the journalist.
– Do you happen to know who that was?
– Mr Bloom, what do you think of me?

Bloom stumbled, the sides of his face grew hot until he spoke, simperingly :

– I think you are a man of faith, honourable.
– I would prove so by not giving out the names of those who walk these grounds. If I was to do the same with you what would you think?

Mistake coming here. Last night : still dreaming perhaps. Bloom stepped back from the door, his raised hand of farewell falling in a gesture that seemed to offer the land back to the clergyman. The voice called after him, a portentous pastiche of the man in the mackintosh :

– Admit no messengers, receive no tokens.

Bloom raised his hand again, as if in salutation to the wisdom. His foot slipped on the moss-covered edge of a stone. Hopeless. Must get outside : twice in two days is twice too much.

As he walked to the gates the priest's words followed him :

– Find where truth is hid, though it were hid indeed within the centre.

As he walked from the gates of the cemetery his right shoulder clattered the bladed shoulder of a thinner, younger man, who was occupied with the reading of a book. The man rebounded from Bloom, who apologised, and continued reading. He walked through the gates of the cemetery towards the Parishioner's Office. Two men of the same age, anxious and intent in their pursuit, followed closely behind the man in black as he walked.

```
You are standing outside the cemetery gates.
You have one life remaining.

?S
>GOTO 67

?Follow the man in black.
>GOTO 154
```

AEOLUS »   ⬚ X

*Act 3, Scene 1: A Room in the castle / Inside Bloom's head
[next page: The Fertility of the Question]. 12pm*

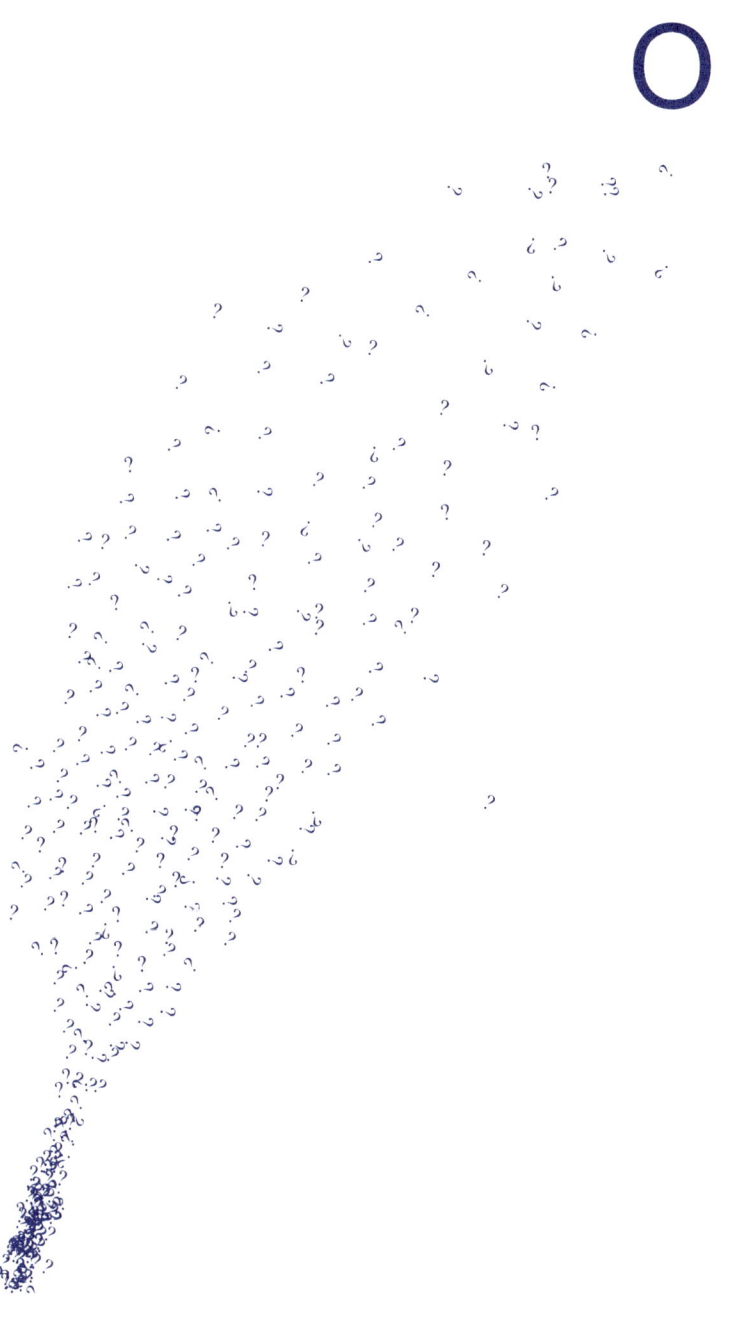

You can see the River. Brilliant way to check if
you?re H/A/P/P/Y. Barclays would drown you in
the Liffey if they knew you?d clicked on this
link.

?must eat, day getting the better of me
>GOTO 71

?start level 2
>GOTO 155

LESTRYGONIANS

Act 3, Scene 2: A hall in the castle / Ormond Quay. 1pm

Feel quite peckish after that. Peck peck. Like a hen, all the same really, feel the need and put your beak in. Peck. Pick. Pock. Puck. Put *Pack* before, then get all the vowels, see : Pack Peck Pick Pock Puck. Must eat, day getting the better of me.

Along College Green the city was stirring with midsummer life : afternoon excursions and conversations, evening plans becoming facts. The sun had lowered into a steady hum of trotting hackneys and human voices. Occasionally, through it all, a song tumbled out onto the street or a lone drunk cried for his mother. The young man at the gates, I wonder what it was he was reading? Words, words, words. Must write to Milly too. Ah, that's it : he had a look of Alec Bannon. Slightly older perhaps.

Lemoncurd crumpets. Spiced orangeblossom. Caramel pears. Scent and salivation plumed through the thoughts of Bloom. Maybe buy some buns, walk down to the quay. No : gulls. They'll remember from yesterday. Hooked beaks clean out the pockets. Imagine the headline on that : Homeless man seeks night in nest. Winged usurper deprives gulls of lunch. Bunsnatcher last seen running towards Temple Bar.

Should have known M'intosh was working, why else would he be there? Doomed for a certain term to walk the night. Sour breath he had, as if munching on fungus. No doubt quite the narcotic. Soil on his lips too. Crumbs of the earth. Could just eat that Davy Byrne's sandwich again. Might have sold out : all the gorgonzola is gone. Gone, the gorgonzola. Wine too. Earth and blood. Wonder how it feels the day after, if that metempsychosis I told Molly about is true? Take a while to find out where everything is, just like working with a new client. Kettle there? Mind if I sit?

Hunger growled in Bloom's stomach. Phoo, stomach like a wheel crank. Light breakfast no good you see, leaves you quite exposed. Couldn't touch a morsel after that chat with Molly. Little bitch she said. Strong words. Feelings? Jealous even? Green eyed monster. Not Molly : dark Spanish eyes. First thing I noticed. Then buttocks, more than breasts even. Wonder why that is? Largest muscle. Strengthens the heart. Seat of all passions. Part both men and women have. Wider in women of course.

Bloom cut up Crown Alley to the Temple Bar. Markets bustling with business. Alongside a stall a man was trading Asian teapots, deep pigments firing into glossed ceramics. The restaurants stirred with casual workers, stained hands on hard white bread. The scent of food mingled with the flickering fumes of cigar and stale beer. Couldn't stomach here, not today. Will cross. Had enough hand to mouth. Soaps for sale, a penny less than Sweny's. Charged me extra for messing him around with that potion. Hunger. Feel like people can see through you. Young Dedalus after the porter, in a heap with his ashplant. Like a ghost. Less than. Needs to eat more, wouldn't touch a morsel. Grief does that. Eats what you don't eat. Eats its own tail. Cycles. The inner tube has no mouth.

Across the Temple Bar cantering jarveys passed as patient Bloom paused. He died of hunger, under a horse. Wonder if that's where it comes from : could eat a horse? Worth dying for. Foo, no. Meat far too tough. Like that time Molly cooked steak, left a niggling root in my jaw for months.

He crossed the Liffey, gulls circling his head with screams. After scraps again. Getting to know me. Must be careful, follow me home.

He looked down at the weedy walls of the river. Low tide, warm summer. Can see the base here. Littered with claypipes. Little messages to the future. More chance of finding the Road to Damascus than seeing a fish down there. Fried sole. Peppered mackerel. Battered deep fried cod doused with malt vinegar.

Along Ormond Quay the smell of frying chateaubriand teased Bloom's nostrils. Could treat myself today. After yesterday, could do with. Just a bite. He eyed the menu in the window. Single tenderloin with pomme fritte, two shillings. Could buy Molly those stockings for that. As he walked on a man in white smocks looked out through the glass. Ready for service. Bloom tipped his hat : a white shred of text fell flakewhite to the floor. ~~HENRY FLOW.~~ My. The envelope. Forgot. Have a look at my secret name. Must be more careful. He picked up the paper and pinched it to a ball. Must be more careful. What if Molly? Now I've said he should address her as my wife does she know I know? She knows I know she knows. I know she knows I know she knows. And the fire in her against my letter to Martha! Could she not care and feel so strongly? There's hope in the tour idea yet. A holiday for us, find each other again. And Stephen : we could look after him.

He moved on from the steakhouse window. The waiter watched, his face a white disc on the coatstand of wellserviced shoulders. Bloom walked along the Ormond Quay. Not too far he thought, will end up at the cabman's shelter. At least we paid. Don't fancy that sailor again, smelt like yesterday's dinner. Most of it in his beard in fact. Must finish that conversation with Stephen, catch him while he's sober. The British tour could be wonderful, do us both a favour. Whole tour of the British Isles, I could teach him Hebrew, he could work on my Latin.

A grey cloud passed with crosshatching sunlight across the pavement. Stains on her sheets there were. Cream pearls. Must have. No. Lunch first. Empty stomach empty mind. How about? Bloom read the menu in the deli doorway. Avocado, chili, garlic salt on bloomer. Humous salad. Celeriac soup. Celeriac. Sounds of the words, describes what it is, almost. Chink of spoon on ceramic : celeriac soup. Fine recipe I had for that once, from Mrs Josephs. Came off well, the year Milly was born. Cooked more then. Ambitious.

Bloom entered the clattering Food Hall. Nice array of buns. Waitress too, like an hourglass. Prefer some meat. Less of a snack. Impressive buffet here, pick and choose what you like.

The foodhall buzzed with expectant diners. Spoons clinked, cups clattered, forks forked. Above all was the steady swell of summertime chatter. Bloom breathed. Nice to be out after that chat with Molly. Quite stifling. Still, had to address it. The train can't leave the station in silence. Perhaps this is the start of better times? Make it back somewhere close to where we were.

Music rose through Bloom's buoyant mood. *Down at Margate looking very charming you are sure to meet.* That girl on the beach yesterday. Had me in quite a pickle. *Those girls, dear girls, those lovely seaside girls.* Male thing that is : eat before someone else does. Fill your face. Couldn't walk on until I felt the moment had passed. At least I got to. Before she limped. *With sticks they steer and promenade the pier to give the boys a treat.* Poor thing, wonder if she thought I knew and looked on in any case. *In pique silks and lace, they tip you quite a playful wink.* Hope for love at least. Others like her perhaps. Coupleup. *In bloomers smart they captivate the heart when cycling down the prom.* Pass on to their children perhaps? No, doesn't work like that. Used to buy bloomers for Molly. Liked those clocks on the side of them? Why I wonder? Draws the eye to the slightest flesh. Makes more naked to be covered. What was that poem I liked?

Give me my mistress as she is,
Dressed in her naked simplicities

Herrick. That's it. Strange how the passion travels over time. Body hollowed out by now, bones foxscavenged. Worms don't care. I turned quite a sonnet in my time, do you mind? Munchmunch.

Ah service, yes :

– What do you have that has meat? Not too heavy.
– Veal sandwich?
– Yes, veal sandwich. Yes. And a lemonade please.

No wine today. Mistake that was. Understandable after the funeral but did me no good. Keep a clear mind in case Molly wants to talk later. Wonder if I can make them do the tour? Perhaps set up an encounter between them and see if they take the bait. Take them to a show : talk about what might be a good thing for us all. See themselves as someone else. Logic of critique, then : there you are. Talked themselves into it. Quite a mousetrap.

Bloom stared towards the window as an antique sunlight streamed through the bleachwhite nets. A pottage of white clouds streamed above. Does each one have a shape? Quite like a dog that one. The other : needle and cotton. Sleepily watching blurry Bloom eased into a daydream.

... Stephen and Molly enter together, tenderly. Molly kneels and makes a show of protestation unto him. He takes her up and declines his head upon her neck : lays him down in a bank of flowers : she, seeing him asleep, leaves him. Boylan comes in, takes off his crown, kisses it, and pours poison in Stephen's ear, and exits. Molly returns; finds Stephen dead,

and makes passionate action. The Poisoner, with some two or three Mutes, comes in again, seeming to lament with her. The dead body is carried away. The Poisoner woos the Queen with gifts : she seems loath and unwilling awhile, but in the end accepts his love ...

A clatter of wood drew Bloom's attention to the door : HELYS' sandwichmen. Must be why they call them that. Eat what they are. Men full of sandwiches. Wonder if they'll share a plate like they share the word? H takes the first bite, followed by E, L, Y, then S sniffs up the crumbs. How long did I work there? Four, no, five years. After Papli died. Whole adult life come to think of it. Wonder if I was unhappy about it more then? Too young to know he wasn't coming back. Long time dead : makes sense now. Thought the next day was a long time then. Impatience. Imperthnthn thnthnthn. Pang of bad air then. Surely not? Man next to me. Let off as he eats. In one end out the other. Looks like the eggsalad he's having too. Worse tomorrow. Think it would dampen the appetite. No. Down the hatch. Chicks fill the nest, then leave. Ban potpourri. Have that, I'm done. Wouldn't mind saying something. Think twice next time. Bad digestion breeds good manners. At least go to the bathroom. Close a door on it.

Outside, the man in black who he'd seen entering the cemetery earlier was walking briskly, followed by the same two men and the priest, conferring as they moved. Oldfashioned dress. Wonder what? Some papal discussion? Fancydress engagement.

Bloom looked closely at a poster on the wall. *Marmite*. Strange taste it has. Like metal and leather. Wonder if it would improve with Guinness? Could do a decent jingle on that. 'Black by day, black by …' Oo, good one. Must write it down. Approach them even. Careful to send to myself in an envelope. Maybe add something else about light. 'What is it in Tequila? Wormwood, wormwood, those lovely glowing worms of night.' Too much telling in advertising these days. Best to be your own best judge : becomes instinct like that. Have to suit the words to what you're trying to sell, can't do it the same second time round. Have to be subtle too, hold a person's reflections so they see it and think they saw it first. Seen too many adverts bellowing for cash : puts people off.

With a steady careful hand Bloom took a pen and ripping a slip of envelope from his pocket wrote :

Black by day, black by night.
L. Bloom, 17 June 1904.

```
You are holding an ENVELOPE addressed to your-
self.

?Follow the man in black.
>GOTO 79

?Think what I could do for Molly with what that
money would buy. Mollybuy Molibi Molify fo fum.
>GOTO 156
```

SCYLLA AND CHARYBDIS

*Act 3, Scene 3: A room in the castle /
a brothel in Monto. 2pm*

Stephen Dedalus entered the afternoon whorehouse, headbowed and unrepentant. A giltedged edition of Aristotle's *Poetics* curled in the tight sidepocket of his jacket. Leave rhetoric at the door. Forms detach from forms : lust knows no ideals. The ache is in the detail.

Saturdays : a year of his life had been spent in dedication to the Blessed Virgin Mary. Under the larchdrip of rain the day still came to him in the colour blue. Blue with a flutter of white cloud. Along the corridor there was a smell of fetid horsedung. And urine : the scent he had tested his faith by. More brothels in Dublin than Paris. Drink until we're arse-over-tip Mulligan had said and like an acolyte he'd followed. Now it was the next day, a day when something meaningful might actually happen. At the whorehouse alone it would be crushing not to touch another.

He followed the yellow corridor four doors down, knocked without waiting and entered. The woman sat with her back to him, her face looking out from the oval rim of the silvering mirror. She spoke :

– You're early.
– Lust has no concept of time, Blake's angels are Nereids.
– Did you bring the liquor?

Stephen pulled a slim bloodred phial from the opposite pocket to Aristotle. He reached across her palewhite shoulders and placed the bottle on the dresser. A tear of rich tannins ran down the glass. Blood on the rosewood. He remembered his delinquent dalliance : after daydreaming of Mercedes for hours he would sit on the edge of his mother's bed and stare into her dressing mirror. Was the sadness of that time born from the chafing of having to leave mother for a woman he was yet to meet? Now she's gone : for what? The earth spun in a shower of dustmotes. Poets sing fruitlessly towards deaf galaxies.

There was a smell in the room of old ash and cinnamon. A hint of juniper. On the wall was a picture of John the Baptist and further along, where the nubs of the candles dimmed, was the outline of the Blessed Virgin. He sat on the edge of the crumpled sheets as his mother's face whitened inside the dim oval. No, not here. Gertrude get out. This is the tragedy of a sunken rut.

He looked at the woman in front of him, her blushpink flesh sunk back to the skeletal grey of his mother. Eyes blackened to cavities.

– No, I can handle the Bard but not Sophocles.

She turned to look at him : Stephen sat with his head held in a tangle of thin arms.

– Act 3, Scene 4, the Queen's closet.
– I'm no queen sweetheart. Did you bring the money?
– I have money.
– For last time too?
– And next. Take what you need.

Stephen drew a tight roll of inkstained banknotes from his pocket and threw it beside her on the bed. Forgot the library slips. Must go back. Here first, words later.

The whore took the money and walked to the wall. She lifted the sacred image of the Virgin : a secret alcove lay behind. Stephen watched as she put the money inside, alongside a lead pipe :

– I set you up a glass where you may see the inmost part of yourself.
– Drink?
– Pour me some.

She turned to pour. A rat scurried from beneath a far dresser to the corner of the room.

– Dead, for a ducat, dead!
– Drink this.

The dark drink tasted of faroff earth : the flattened grove of the continent. It calmed him. The face of the girl at the gate of the beach came to him. *Do you like the poetry of Yeats?* There was poetry in Dublin, and hope. Georgina Johnson, whore of Monto, slipped her hand into Stephen's foxed and boozestained shirt. He grabbed her wrist :

– After this drink I must go. I came to pay you back, not to increase my debt.

She laughed. Another boy unsure of himself. There was something else with him, a different kind of desperation that marked him out from the others who came here. Stephen was aware she'd noticed : he allowed her to watch as he took a crumpled library slip from his pocket. A whiling away of an hour, a forgotten exercise. A few days before, Haines and Mulligan had disappeared without him – a portent of the pending abandonment – and he'd sat at the kitchen table in the tower, searching *Hamlet* for each reference to Denmark then writing it onto the page. He then changed, by hand, each reference to Denmark to Dublin. He pulled the dewyellow paper from his pocket and read this strange poetic work as she combed her hair still facing the mirror.

THE TRAGEDY OF HAMLET, PRINCE OF DUBLIN

In which the majesty of buried Dublin
Did sometimes march? by heaven I charge thee, speak!

Than is the throne of Dublin to thy father.

From whence though willingly I came to Dublin,
To show my duty in your coronation,

Good Hamlet, cast thy nighted colour off,
And let thine eye look like a friend on Dublin

Why, 'tis a loving and a fair reply:
Be as ourself in Dublin. Madam, come;
This gentle and unforced accord of Hamlet
Sits smiling to my heart: in grace whereof,
No jocund health that Dublin drinks to-day

                        which is no further
Than the main voice of Dublin goes withal

Something is rotten in the state of Dublin

          the whole ear of Dublin
Is by a forged process of my death
Rankly abused:

Let not the royal bed of Dublin be
A couch for luxury and damned incest.

That one may smile, and smile, and be a villain;
At least I'm sure it may be so in Dublin:

There's ne'er a villain dwelling in all Dublin
But he's an arrant knave.

Dublin's a prison.

A goodly one; in which there are many confines, wards and dungeons, Dublin being one o' the worst.

It is not very strange; for mine uncle is king of Dublin

                           O, my old
friend! thy face is valenced since I saw thee last: comest thou to beard me in Dublin?

How can that be, when you have the voice of the
                                                                          king
himself for your succession in Dublin?

SCENE IV. A plain in Dublin.

Where is the beauteous majesty of Dublin?

Why, here in Dublin; I have been sexton here,
                man and boy, thirty years

Larded with many several sorts of reasons
Importing Dublin's health and England's too,
With, ho! such bugs and goblins in my life

Your lordship is right welcome back to Dublin.

Richer than that which four successive kings
In Dublin's crown have worn.

Stephen drained his glass. The whore was back at the picture of the Virgin Mary, removing a few sheaths from the roll of muddy notes inside the hole in the wall. Curiosity drew him back to his surroundings.

– What's that?
– In case of trouble.
– I'm not here for trouble.
– I can tell that by your voice.
– Howso?
– It's softer than most men of your age.
– I suckle daily at my dead mother's breast –
– Herethere, nownow …

The whore unstrapped the offwhite strap from her shoulder. A scent rose from her, as if through a shroud, of jasmine and cloves : a delicate and sinful perfume. I must play king to myself : execute my own exile. Europe will be my England : the book I will write will be my wax seal. There is no majestic body through which Dublin decays. Discipline is needed for late nights, there are stars breathing in these tannins. But will she come again, the girl who stitches pages?

A rat ran out from the frowsy curtain and detecting its observers turned quickly to the dressing table. It wedged its body in the narrow aperture between the wood and the wall unable to propel itself fully into the hidden space. Stephen surprised the whore with his speed : in one wristquick move he was on his feet with his ashplant whipping the rear of the animal into a nervous mass of blackened blood. He punctuated each blow with what seemed like an incomprehensible curse, a language constructed from obscure Latin and expressions gleaned from the gutter : *Obosomblackasdeatholimedsouldthatstrugglingtobefreeartmoreengagedhelpangelsmakeassay...*

Georgina Johnson watched the man she'd praised for his gentleness beat the rat repeatedly with tight-lipped authority. The rat stopped moving, its nervous system finally silenced, as Stephen continued whipping with the ferrule tip of his cane. Its body began to unform, separating like loam into discrete portions.

Stephen sat back on the bed, his body fighting for composure, righting itself through deep convulsions :

– I am being pursued by another book. I have seen a valid hero on the ramparts of the place I live in. Between the ghost of my mother and this figure in black, peace is an impossibility … My mother stays : this physic but prolongs thy sickly days.

The prostitute watched him, curious and perplexed.

– I will leave now. There are two women in white in my life : one of whom might yet still be real to me.

He disappeared through the door he'd entered an hour earlier, his arms and legs in flailing imitation of the spider that watched, with mathematical patience, above the door. Georgina Johnson shouted after him :

– Here, you've left your poem on the bed …

```
19 memes as plump as Buck Mulligan! You won?t
even recognise the last one!!!
>GOTO 87

Stephen Dedalus is 22 and looks unbelievable!!!
>GOTO 157
```

WANDERING ROCKS

*Act 3, Scene 4: The Queen's closet /
Central Dublin 1904 and 2014. 3pm*

FATHER CONMEE : Ah, the urchin, another dispossessed. Waste, waste. Still, the answers come later. For now, perseverance. Another day today : no funerals I know of. His father always so bereft of shoes.

YOUNG MASTER DIGNAM : Found Pa's shoes. Ma never saw them. Might fit me one day, shooting up all the time he said. Eat me greens. He never did : potatoes and the black stuff, Ma said. Wonder why the black stuff made his nose go red? Poor Pa. Mostly singing though he was.

STEPHEN DEDALUS : Stephen, singing, looked at the darkening hood of the clouds. Chafed flesh pleased him. A poem stirred behind his conscience : a maggot in a textblock. Gave the whore too much. Yesterday's winnings and a florin from my wages. More than the Bard's secondbest bed.

MOLLY BLOOM : Molly with quick evenhand pressed flat the rumpled bedsheets. Two commasized tears of sexwet fluids punctuated the clean linen. Some cheek he had saying he should address me as his wife well yes he was right there did you see his face though when I asked about that little bitch couldn't look away quick enough was glad the cat came in what kind of man is he anyway the way he was writing to her and making up a whole basket of shit about her being some kind of writing assistant Poldy knows stuff but he's not a writer too practical he is pulls himself back from going too deep a good practical mind and curious too I like that in him but at his age saying he's going to start writing who's he kidding he likes the idea no doubt being looked up to by younger men and women coming up to him asking if he could give advice on how to make their sentences sing O yes he'd love that would be out to all hours soaking it up while I stayed at home wondering where he was huh some idea he has of me thinking I could live like that at least Boylan deals with the here and now and wants me in front of the audience never thought in all my life and the way he showed me with the fruit the dripping peaches Goodness and it's still only afternoon enough time to make it again if he comes back from where he's had to go so quick after taking it out can still feel it inside me wouldn't think it would be able to but that's nature I suppose I remember that gynaecologist I met saying if you can imagine all the space in the hallway once you've got the parcel through the box guess that's it must be after two children let's not think of that not yet too soon and still wet he is inside me that smell like chemicals almost a kind of warm cleanliness to it would take it all anywhere he liked perhaps not the mouth no do that once and they want it all the time just another trick to pull off still nice the first time then you wonder what's it in for yourself it's nice to be had of course but want to feel it too get all the filth with the release then not just an idea or something for him to add to his trophy cabinet.

ENTER GHOST OF STEPHEN'S MOTHER : I am behind the trophy cabinet Stephen. Schnuuufff. Your hair needs washing. Each morning you let me, even after you'd started at the university. Schnuuuffff. It was the only time you would listen, stooped over the sink, head in the water as you were at the baptismal font. Chrisms of gold in your hair. Schnuuuuffff. There is still time, Stephen, for you to pray for me. I will sleep then. Step between me and my fighting soul. Free me from this closet. Schhnuuuffff. I am still here for the resolution. The body is thrown to sea.

BUCK MULLIGAN : The body like a trophy from the sea. Good job I was there to catch it, trained as well to pump it back to life if needed. Kinch the coward. He'll have good reason to turn to drink next time I see him, vomiting on a dead man's head : a metaphor for his tired verse. Hoist by his own petard. That will hit. I wonder if the *Dublin Evening Mail* will write that piece on me : MALACHI MULLIGAN BRINGS DEAD MAN TO PEACE.

YOUNG DUBLIN MOTHER : Not exactly peace but happiness. Bingboooing. Listen to that tannoy Billy! More apple? No. No Ta. Say No Ta. Funny how it changed us, me and

Si. Knew every pub in Dublin at one point. He'd guard the bushes as I took a pee under the stars. Carry me to the stairs. Another piece of apple Billy? Thought we'd take it with us. In our stride. More than that. What's that Billy, bingbooooing! Little Billy brought that old life crashing down. Couldn't imagine our lives without him now. Built something else between us, me and Si, around little Billy. Not that we wouldn't like to fuck off to the pub every now and again. Time for that later. Stars seem bright enough without eight pints of Guinness in our eyes. Billy, more apple?

RYANAIR HOSTESS OVER DUBLIN AIRPORT : Apple cheeks he said. Three hours later I was giving him head. Monaco again next month. Might take time off there. *She went to work and never came back.* What a story! I see his face as I run through exits : two at the back, four at the centre (two left, two right) and two at the front. His thick fingers running the steps of my back, up, up. Life vests are kept in the overhead locker and will appear in an emergency. Block on the plastic toggle for attention, pull the chord in the event of an evacuation. God, his cock, so long and thick. Emergency lights will flash red. If doors don't open in an emergency make use of the hammers provided.

BOY SCOUT LEADER ON DUBLIN BUS : Hammers and pegs we need. Can't forget. Show the younger ones they've got to think ahead. Expect to get there and their tents are pitched for them. Was the same when I started. Good to see on their shoulders though : 3rd 40th 41st DUBLIN GROUP DONNYBROOK 1927 SACRED HEART OF ULLAMH.

Red shawls around their necks. Hardest bit's when their mates drop out and they want to stick to it, through the teasing and the jeers. If you believe it, do it, is what I say. Must be cruel, only to be kind. They decide themselves. Got hopes for Frederick, only thirteen but he's got the right kind of enthusiasm. That's all it takes : dedication, the right kind of hammer for the pegs. And curiosity.

PUB LANDLORD : Curiosity killed the cat. And a thousand fuckin' drunks. Not sure how many more I can scoop up from the floor. Developed quite a good line in it so I have : *We're worried about you! Just want to get you home in one piece!* All these people here don't want to see you like this. (Green snot runnin' down your fuckin' nose like the Gulf Stream whippin' up the Liffey). *Here you go, here's a cab. This'll see you right!* Then watch him mumblin' somethin' about his mother as he gets in the back seat. This one the other week couldn't even speak then I pops him in the back of the cab and instead of puttin' on a seatbelt he starts fidgetin' tryin' to get porn up on his laptop.

I.T. HELPDESK ADVISOR : This laptop's a pain in the hole. You'll need to log in with a different password. Pain. In. The. Hole. I can't sort it out, I'm on holiday, get in touch with Neil. Ask him for the four digit pin. You can't get into the domain on the laptop. Ask Neil for the VPM connection, you'll get the remote access then. I don't know why, they're funny that way. That's the thing. Let's push for a change to save fucking around with secure IDs. *Helllo,* you there. *Helllo?*

DRINKER IN THE HAIRY LEMON : Hello Dan he says and he catches my eye then we're on the second pint. I only came out for the paper. Won't stay long. By then John Barry and Steve arrive and we're talking about power and I'm giving them my views on communication, that the more time you use the phrase 'your thoughts?' in a difficult situation the more leeway there is for resolution. Pete comes in and I nod to him, so he knows I know what he's been up to. Here's Blazes Boylan I say. He smiles and says : more Paddy fuckin' Dignam.

MAN IN THE RÔLE OF SWENY THE PHARMACIST, KENNEDY'S BAR : Dignam would be a treat. Molly's soliloquy it is. How do you think it feels being dressed as the pharmacist from Sweny's seven days of the blinkin' week? Was it for this the clay grew tall? – And yes, you can take this and put it in your pipe : I always preferred the English poets. Guess what, then poetry can make sense! I've never even read the whole of the blinkin' book and here I am taking fictional requests for tinctures : almondoil, benzoin, orangeblossom flower.

WOMAN IN THE RÔLE OF MOLLY BLOOM, KENNEDY'S BAR : Flower of the mountain Yes, I *am* Molly when I perform here, as well him as another, I would. Yes, my mountain flower, I *am* Molly when I read it hot under the white and red light, the audience held there, waiting on my words, his heart beating like mad, and nobody knows I work as a teaching assistant by day, no, not when I'm Molly, the words rolling from me like a mountain mist and I know I'm a woman, Yes, and Joyce drank here once too, in this room, Kennedy's Bar, and would he have liked the way I do it? I think so, the natural way they come from me, Molly's words.

BUILDER IN DUBLIN BOOKMAKERS : Wordsmith in the 4:15, it's a cert. Blinkers for the first time and carrying 5lb less than the favourite. Everything's conspiring towards it, even the guy in the Paddy Power, writer-type, hoping the 'luck of the Irish' will rub off on his literary break, was asking what the odds were. I told him before Old Red behind the counter got a chance. 14-1 it is. Then I watched him fill out his slip, thinking he might risk something big on it and I watch him write in slanted poetic italics : *1 Euro eachway Wordsmith Galway 4.15.* Fuck me I'm a builder and I've got a 100 times that on it and that'll sort out the stag night this weekend when it comes in flying like a shot off a shovel.

MAN AT THE CHILLS CONCERT,
THE BUTTON FACTORY : Shovel did it. Lost an eye in '84, the year The Smiths brought out their first album. *It's time the tale were told of how you took a child and made him old.* Strains my neck trying to hide it, leaning to me left. Mum tells me not to worry, accept it, she says, *You're 53 for goodness' sake.* As if I need a mother to remind me of that! What a gig, the few who remember the proper '80s bands. Is 'Pink Frost', or is it not, the best song of the era? Faux Irish like Bono getting big on the Bunnymen sound and fucking off to America, trading in the green flag of their homeland for folds of red rusty notes. Best band in the world? Can't see it meself.

TWEET : I had a dream that @PaoloNutini played for the Dublin team, midfield. I never thought I could ever imagine that! I love my dreams.

TWEET : I was 18 years old when I went down to Dublin with a fistful of money and a cartload of dreams.

TWEET : Flying home for Christmas : Tears of joy and laughter as Irish troops touch down in Dublin.

```
What?s happening? You are somewhere in Central
Dublin.

?Check for updates and reboot
>GOTO 95

?Start task manager
>GOTO 158
```

SIRENS

*Act 4, Scene 1: A room in the castle /
public toilets, Temple Bar. 4pm*

Tinkle untainted, gold and bronze.
Bloomsound, a tinkle, sighing sound.
Both he thought, blazes and cider.
Unfurling lightcoil, blooming.
Pearls of maidenhair, plash and silent roar.
Let off a little, silent hiss.
Fro and to, protuding titbit.
Coiling flower, lidless, trembling foils of aqua.
*Down the Liffey, light on rapids, torn throwaway
    sails passed sibilant quays.*
Small Rudy, sighs of Bloom. Lived to see.
    Allworlds of possibles, flowing.
Curling endstops, bronze by gold.
Purls, at push, last blast of kidneyjuice.
A throstle. A thrush. Wonder if?
No. No for yes, is lost.
Pearls of semen on the sheets.
Echo. Answer sweet.
Surrender. Lost. Swurls.
Lemon soap a relief.

The warm the joy the feel.
Stops and starts. Alluring, ah!
Letter I must. Sounds it is.
Love. Love's answers.
Mush of seeds and eyes.
Kiss before the.
Words? Music?
Molly's potion then Stephen.
Check the undead Dedalus.
Molly's potion, then Stephen
thinks thinks of Dedalus.
Check the undead afterflows.
Check, endstop. Quiver.
Done!

Zeazlack
Pickzuccubuz
Uptrouzclung
Zeazlack
Zealfat
Whalefeed
To teach
Zeaslack
Up
Zeazlack
Bazzcent
Abzmoke
Zhakepass
Up
Taverntrawl
Dallydance
Zeazlack

FuForFreeFroFoFPheiFaf
PhePhaFaForFaFirFallPhe
FelForOfFoeFaOfPheRef
PheEfiEfiPheFielIfEfiPhe

Shoe
    Sose
  Sterold
Steerlish
    Swunrunk
Swithshy
   Stillslips
  Shocliq
    Sintheis
Staceshould
    Smashsin
Sseachchor
   Seachseem
 Shorestill
    Shailings
  Shonesea
  Shepasspassshe
  Shalus
Shologise
   Shonciousscent
Slushedface
 Sweavesheak
Shubstantialush

Platomb mouth
To mouth
DouBloom
Eagerears
Curious for
Pussenwords
Who brollow
Melopetry
Stoubled
Tinslence
Wollow trough
Of norse toge
This life
Mead wok
Pacross
Ded swords
His sour
O
Of wards

{gust of wind}

HeighHo! HeighHo!
PeckPock! PeckPock!
PickPuck! PickPuck!
PutPack! PutPack!
PockPuck! PockPuck!
CurdCrump! CurdCrump!
PearQuay! PearQuay!
HookBeak! HookBeak!
MulchFung! MulchFung!
NarcSoil! NarcSoil!
WheelCrank! WheelCrank!
HeapPlant! HeapPlant!
PhooTwo! PhooTwo!
BloomFlow! BloomFlow!
SheKnows! SheKnows!
SheKnows! SheKnows!
SheKnows! SheKnows!
SheKnows! SheKnows!

rcraacArucocr

rcraacArucocr

rcraacArucocr

rcraacArucocr

rcraacArucocr

rcraacArucocr

rcraacArucocr

rcraacArucocr

rcraacArucocr

almondoil, benzoin, orangeblossom
almozoin bendoil angeossom
mossolgar zoildo milmoss
loinzin loben molrange
mindil lossmoin zildo
eosgil blonoin onoil
doilben inora som
olgar moil loss
inz oil orage
miz en ge

miz en ge
inz oil orage
olgar moil loss
doilben inora som
eosgil blonoin onoil
mindil lossmoin zildo
loinzin loben molrange
mossolgar zoildo milmoss
almozoin bendoil angeossom
almondoil, benzoin, orangeblossom

COME PLEAT

CYCLOPS

Act 4, Scene 2: Another room in the castle /
Barney Kiernan's pub. 5pm

There
e was his slick
pale yellow jewsbody
lurching through the city, his
sticky jewseye all over the fish
and books. Death of the nation he
said I'll give him death and anything he thinks we should toler
ate his freedom of expr
ression well that's
his view

g. I
bet he's got
a head full of num-
bers, always counting.
Who's drinking water and
who's drinking wine, by
Gob it makes me sick.
At the bar did you
speaks a

              Throw-
         away, he has it
       to burn let me tell you.
     Money goes to money,
    leaves tne rest of us picking
    crumbs from the biscuit-
     box. And the physog
      on him too, like a
        bloody good deal
             rank dog

Won't
take a drink
like a real man
so he won't, cigar
smoking in his
hand

about
Irish his-
tory, he'got t
o be joking,
devi

rned-
up   Jew
ent to the
nose

NAUSICAA

*Act 4, Scene 3: Another room in the castle /
Priest's house facing Sandymount Strand. 8pm*

Cuckoo, cuckoo : the cock. The cock crowed in the Canon O'Hanlon's house as he looked through the window at the perfect form of the man on the shore. Such a build as he walked. Who was he? Of course it was wrong for a priest to desire and if he must desire then of course a woman it should be, like the Bible says, only best to keep distance. The grille of the confessional is there for a reason. Yet Father O'Hanlon had always been drawn to men, even those of his own cloth. The silent hush over soda bread and fried mutton chops as the silence rose, ascended even, into something more than words could say. Beyond the cloth was safer, and there was no harm in looking out, wondering about the wanderer, as he strode lazily dreamily towards Sandycove. He was not one of his congregation, of that he was certain. He would have recognised the olive complexion, the perfectly symmetrical moustache. What was he carrying? Ah, a bag from Sweny's chemists. Father O'Hanlon brought to his senses the imagined scent of lemon, orange and talc : scents he liked on another man. They rose in heat in weather like this, ascending with subdued but present sweat. The man bent to pick up something from the shore. A sensitive type, one who would appreciate the beauty in everything he had to offer, the small details that surrounded them everywhere, distinct and resplendent. With guiltshyselfawareness Canon O'Hanlon felt the blood rush to his tightclothed organ. Cuckoo, cuckoo. He pictured the man on his bed, legs parted, inviting him to a dark secret world of flesh and saliva. A master perhaps : he must do as he wanted. He moved the curtains slightly wider to follow the man's journey towards the Martello Tower. In time the man would come to know every inch of his body, that body controlling his own earthly paradise, the bristles along his nipples : to lick, to suck, to play. There would be tensions and eruptions and afterwards he would wash his hair, yes, wash away his own bodily memories that had seemed to cleanse him new like a spring welling from beneath the skin, rising from the heart's pulsations. Canon O'Hanlon felt his own hand lower into the tightblack cloth of his trousers. All came loose. The man was becoming distant. Canon O'Hanlon walked with lassoed ankles to find the binoculars he used for spotting curlews and gulls along the shore and aimed them at the distancing figure of the man, receding shorewards towards Sandycove. Just once, one time, to feel their keen sweat mingle in an aura distinct to them. He wanted to please and by pleasing, please God. Could there be a case in that? He pictured the bedposts, four towers that he himself owned in his own private sanctuary, adding a fifth, a sixth. God saw all of course, but perhaps a blind eye he would turn to this. The whole of Canon O'Hanlon's longlistening life had been spent on others. To reclaim this one thing back would lift the tension, renew him for further good works. Was it too much? He stroked himself. The distancing man became bigger in his mind, more abundant in every aspect, his proportions inconceivably appealing, pulling him towards, pulling. Cuckoo, cuckoo. His taste, all sensations rising, both canarybirds out of their little houses and chirping God, O God, for the first full brightdawn of their longing, yes, just liked he'd imagined it before, only for real now. The bedposts, the sweat and the vibrations of their bodies shaking the earthly foundations around them rose to a showering crescendo of gold and water, a welter of nerves ending in this one true communion never to end because it had been and Canon O'Hanlon watched the canary turn to white water in his hand it was raining outside it must be it was raining it was running down the glass yes it was this once and this once forever. Cuckoo, cuckoo.

...

Wonder who that was in the window? Canon O'Hanlon? Nice man he is. Quiet life it must be too. Reflection, solitude. Must go and say hello some time. Pass an hour. Take a cake.

Mr Bloom kept to the path. Must be careful not to go back. Where was she? Further along the Strand it was. Quite exposed, can see it now. Felt to all the world like just the two of us. Wonder if anyone saw? Let them. No harm, not as if there was anything to see. Just a moment. Summer. Puffs of dust.

This it is, I think. Behind these trees. Strange place to live, a tower. Quite old. Built to fend off the French. Wonder if there's been any history without wars? Had this out in Barney Kiernan's yesterday, nasty sort he was. Thank goodness Cunningham was there. Felt they wanted to kick me off their turf. Took that cigar to give some breathing space. Aggression makes them feel better, like real men. Quite an adventure jumping into that cab after. Still, left a sourtaste in the mouth.

The Martello Tower rose before Bloom like a washpot without a lid. A sandblasted toadstool. The black door at its base was gnome-like, too small for human use, a black flap for a tiny creature of land or sea. He read the text printed like a titlepage in capped emboss: J. BENNETT CHURCHES DUBLIN 1822. Bloom peered inside the oversized mortice lock. A dead spider caught captive in its own silk web. Wonder if he could get back in? He said something last night, I think, about Mulligan having the key and Haines wanting it.

Above the door there was a window of almost the same size, twelve feet from the floor, as if either would be of use for ingress or egress. Bloom noticed that the bricks were out-of-proportion with the size of the structure, misaligned blocks furnaced in amber, beige and grey. A good place to come and think Bloom thought. Shame he has to share it with those other two. Bloom looked up the higher door, a ladder ran down to where he stood, thinking.

He circled to the other side : the same door, only this time surrounded on each side with thick panes of glass. Curious, like blocks of ice. Wonder if it's cold in there? Feel like a prince cast from my own state. Bloom knocked three times. Dullsounding oak echoed back to his knuckles. No chance of that falling. Quite solid. Another window and above that a chimney with two spouts.

Bloom walked the base of the tower, a circling porpoise. He stood beneath the turreted overhang as if a princess might appear, bearing a heaving bosom only his words could silence. He stroked his moustache : nothing. He peered through the small thick panes of flowery glass at the bottom window. The shadow was his shadow. He wiped the dried voiles of cobwebs from his nose. Quite ticklish. In the corner of the glass a louse had turned white and fattened in death : bloated and tortoiselike.

Bloom ran his hand along the wall : rough, compacted oatmeal. His stomach cranked. Perhaps take him for a bite, must be hungry after his excursions? Malnutrition partly responsible for this too. Get him back on the straight. New dawn.

– Who is it you're looking for dear?

An old woman had appeared behind him, her red face pinched into a handrag of curiosity. A chain in her hand : doglead. The doglead leads the dog. Cat eats the fish that eats the worm that the king then eats. Dog eats? Cat. Where is? There. Lurcher. A lurcher lurching.

– A friend of mine.

– Nobody lives here Sweetie!
– Yes, Stephen his name is. He lives with an Englishman and a student doctor.
– Ah no my love this is the wrong tower, you want the one at Sandycove.

The woman pointed towards the curved luscious coastline that hedged the bay. Towards Howth and Molly's seedcake. The lurcher sniffed at Bloom's trousers then mounted his leg, humping in sanddry thrusts.

– No Lancer, down, down boy, leave the nice man!

Bloom walked away from the woman, and the dog, in embarrassed gratitude. Sandycove, right. Still time, close enough to walk? Where are we now, 9pm? Yes, be there by ten. Still time to take him away for an hour. Onwards.

...

```
Bloom. You are back where you started.

?Well, you can?t cross the same river once.
>GOTO 119

?Find the man in black.
>GOTO 161
```

OXEN OF THE SUN

Act 4, Scene 4: A plain in Denmark / outside the Martello Tower and back into Dublin. 10pm

REMEMBRANCE OF THINGS PAST (1913)

For a long time Bloom had gone to bed early. Sometimes when he'd put out the light he would lie with eyes open thinking 'what is sleep?' After an hour he would drift off and dream he had been awake for days. He would wake for real and read a book, Shakespeare sometimes, or *Aspects of the Digestive Tract*. On turning off the light again he would dream of being poisoned and wake with indigestion. Unsure if he was awake or asleep he would say out loud Hamlet's words from the book : *To die, to sleep, perchance to dream*. Molly would elbow him beneath the sheets. The pain would persist outside of the dream, he knew now he was awake, the soft flesh of his shoulders burning. Reality blurred at the edges, as if part of him was the real Prince, lost in Elsinore in search of his father. He looked and was shocked by the darkness as if he'd been blinded. What should have been restful to the eyes felt like a poison and he would look at Molly trying to calm his mind but she was unconscious in the sweet dark matter of sleep.

MRS DALLOWAY (1925)

Mr Bloom thought he would buy Stephen a drink himself.

He had his work cut out. The doors of the tower were tight on their hinges; the city's flotsam surrounding. And then, thought Leopold Bloom, what an evening – fresh as if issued to them on the beach.

What a lark! What a plunge! For so it had always seemed to him, even as he pulled the hinges, which he could hear now, and Stephen burst open the windows above flying into the open air. How enervating, how still, calmer than yesterday the air was this evening; a fillip of the tide; the crash of a wave; cold and sharp (for a man of thirty-eight he was) and solemn, feeling as he did, with Stephen standing above at the open window, he sensed that something awful was about to happen; looking at the beach, looking at the waves, with moisture splashing off them and the crows rising, falling; he remained standing and looking until Stephen said 'Are you delivering vegetables?' – what did he mean? – 'I prefer the devil to vegetables' he added – where was he coming from? He must have stayed indoors since breakfast and only now walked to the terrace. Stephen Dedalus! He had only just come back from Paris, February or March, he forgot which, for his memory was dim, yet it was his sayings one remembered, his eyes, his ashplant, his sneer, his aloofness all remembered long after other's existences had long vanished. How peculiar it was! His sayings like this about vegetables!

He stiffened a little on the beach, waiting for the silence to pass. A charming woman Mrs Purefoy was (knowing her as one does know people who live close to one in Dublin); a touch of the fish about her, the trout, green-blue, lively, though she was nearly forty, and grown a little pale since the birth. There he perched, near where the drowned man was found, never seeing him, waiting to be buried, very stiff.

GONE WITH THE WIND (1936)

Stephen Dedalus was not beautiful but men seldom realized it when caught by his charm unlike other thin students were. In his face were too sharply blended the delicate features of his mother, an aristocrat of Celtic descent, along with the heavy lids of his florid Irish father. But it was an arresting face, pointed of chin, square of jaw. His eyes were pale discs whose burned retinas often stabbed with brisk bad light and were slyly reticent in pubs. Above them, his pinched black hat slanted upward, cutting a startling oblique line against his magnolia-white skin – that skin so primed by Dublin winters and so frequently blushed with pints of ale and occasional gins.

Seated with Bloom in the cool shade of the porch of the tram, his father's scourge, that bright June afternoon of 1904, they made a pretty picture. Mulligan's old patched trousers spread their twined threads of material over his shoes matching exactly the flea-peeled Monto-stained shoes covered with the slops earned from pubs around the Liffey. The hat set off to perfection the seventeen-inch headband, the brightest in three counties, and the tightly pinched brows displayed a history of thoughts well matured for his twenty-two years. But for all the majesty of his spreading fame, the demigodliness of hope netted smugly into a sauvignon or other small whites or any other drink in his lap – his true self was poorly concealed.

The pierced eyes in his white face were troubled, woeful, loamy with liquor, distinctly at variance with Bloom's settled demeanour. Stephen's manners had been imposed upon him by his mother's gentle admonitions and the sterner discipline of her manna : her eyes were his own.

On either side of them, men lounged easily in their seats, squinting at the sunlight through tanned smoke-garnished glass, stared and yawned, their legs crossed, booted to the ankle and thick with polish, socks stained negligently. Thirty-eight years old, five feet seven inches tall, medium in bone and soft in muscle, with oliveskinned face and deep brown hair, Bloom seemed merry and apologetic, his body clothed in the identical suit and breeches as the day before. Both men were as unlike as the bald shepherd to his flock.

Outside, the late afternoon sun slanted down the tram, throwing into gleaming brightness the dogs and children like waste blossoms against the background of new buildings. The town's horses were hitched outside along the driveway, big animals, brown as their masters' sackcloths. Around the horses' legs a pack of lean nervous pigeons quarrelled, their chatter accompanying the carriages to wherever they went. A little aloof, as became an outsider, stood a black-clothed man, hands on the rail, impatiently watching the crowds heading home to supper. 'Fortinbras', he could be heard to say.

1984 (1949)

It was a bright muggy day in June, and the clocks were striking ten. Stephen Dedalus, his chin nuzzled into his breast in an effort to escape the last of the sun, slipped quickly out of the glass doors of the tram, though not swiftly enough to prevent a swirl of grimy dust from entering after him.

The pavement smelt of boiled cabbage and used rag mags. At one end of it a food poster, too large for indoor display, had been pinned to the wall. It depicted simply an enormous potato, more than a metre wide : the face of a potato of about 4.5 ounces, with a heavy black eye and ruggedly contorted features. Stephen made for the stairs of a pub. It was no use trying to resist. Even at the best of times it was seldom worth it and at present the adrenalin current in his blood was cut and ripping through the daylight hours. It was part of the artistic drive in preparation for another week of self-hate. The pub was two flights up and Stephen, who was twenty-two and already had a broken vein in his right nostril, went swiftly, trying to resist several times on the way. On each step, opposite the Liffey, the poster with the enormous potato gazed from the wall. It was one of those pictures which are so contrite that the eyes follow you about when you move. EAT MORE POTATOES, the caption beneath it ran.

Inside the pub a phlegmy voice was reading out a list of numbers which had something to do with horse racing. The voice came from an oblong wooden bench like a shrunken hull which formed part of the fabric of the right-hand wall. Stephen turned the door knob and the voice shrank somewhat, though the words were still distinguishable. The voice (in the Betting Room, it was called) could be avoided but there was no way of shutting it off completely. He moved over to the window : a smallish, fragile figure stood there, the meagreness of her body slightly aggrandised by the blue overalls which were the uniform of the staff. Her hair was very fair, her face unnaturally mercurial, her skin roughened by coarse soap and blue furnace blasts and the heat of the summer's day that was just ending.

Outside, even through the shimmering windowpane, the world looked dark. Down in the street little eddies of wind were whirling dust and torn paper into spirals, and though the sun was gone and the sky a dark black, there seemed to be no colour in anything, except the posters that were plastered everywhere. The pints glazed down from every commanding corner. There was one on the bar immediately opposite. A Guinness harp was fixed to the wall while the dark eyes of the barmaid looked deep into Stephen's own. Down at streetlevel another poster, torn at one corner, flapped fitfully in the wind, alternately covering and uncovering the single word ELIJAH. In the far distance a seagull skimmed down between the tide, hovered for an instant, then flew away again with a curving flight. It was the scavenger flock picking at the leftovers left by the city's people.

Behind Stephen's back the voices of the barmates were still babbling away about horse racing and the under-fulfilment of The Gold Cup. They listened and ignored each other in equal measure. Any move that Stephen made, above the level of a very slight step, would be noticed and, moreover, retained within the field of vision which the Betting Room commanded. There was of course no way of knowing whether he was being watched at any given moment. How often, or on what level, anyone noticed any other individual was guesswork. It was even conceivable that they watched everybody all the time. But at any rate they could tune-in to his mind whenever they wanted to. Stephen had learned to live – did live, from habit that became instinct – in the assumption that every sound he made was overheard, and, except in darkness, every movement scrutinized.

Stephen kept his back turned to the Betting Room. It was safer not to look, as he well knew, even a back can be revealing. A kilometre away the National Library, the place of his true work, towered vast and grey above the grimy landscape. This, he thought with a sort of vague distaste – this was Dublin, chief city of Irish Ore, itself the third most populous of the provinces of Europe. He tried to squeeze out some childhood memory that should tell him whether Dublin had always been quite like this. Were there always these rows of rotting eighteenth-century houses, their sides shored up with banks of bricks, their windows patched with cardboard and their roofs with corrugated iron, their crumbling garden walls sagging in all directions? And the brown sites where the plaster dust swirled in the air and the window-dust star-clustered over the heaps of rubble; and the places where the bins had cluttered a larger patch and there had sprung up sodden towers of wooden dwellings like Lilliput's houses? But it was no use, he could not remember : nothing remained of his childhood except a series of bright-lit epiphanies occurring against the backdrop of over-exerted intelligence.

The National Library – *omphalos,* in Stephenspeak – was startlingly different from any other object in his mind. It was an enormous pyramidal structure of glittering white concrete, soaring up, floor after floor, one thousand metres into the air. From where Stephen stood it was just possible to remember the elegant lettering he'd read a few days back, the three slogans of Francis Bacon:

READING MAKETH A FULL MAN
CONFERENCE A READY MAN
AND WRITING AN EXACT MAN

LOLITA (1955)

Bloom, thorn of Stephen's sleep, light in his eyes. His sire, his son. Bloo-oo-oom : lips pucker tongue blow to the last breath of vowels. Bloo-oo-oom.

He was low, down low, past the noon, standing four-to-five feet outside the pub. He was Bloom in socks. Leopold in slacks. He was Leopold outside the tower. To Stephen's mind he was Leonard, near-Bloom.

Did he have a good opener? He did, he remembered he did. As it went he recalled that he himself like Stephen had bloomed in summer, the man-child in Dublin by-the-sea. Back then? As many years between as was Milly's age now, thereabouts. Dublin's son had grown his own poetic style.

Readers of this unauthorised sequence, outside the pub is one that yesterday misinformed the muse with a lost deposit. The limping muse of hot little blushes. Blushes like buds in his tangled-up thorns.

NAKED LUNCH (1959)

and
start
east

I, Stephen can feel the heat closing in, sense Leonard out there making his move, crunching across dried pigeon stools, drooling praise from Sandycove to Dublin Station, lolling at the turnstile and the iron stairs, ready to coax him via tram away from here ... No longer young, average looking, black hair, a bourgoise feminine kind rattling at the base of the tower door. I am evidently his idea of a writer. You know the kind : tepid with barmaids and hansom cab drivers, talking about mediocre books and false spirituality, calling the pharmacist by his first name. A Dublin bourgoise. Last night before the tram right on time this practical pseud passed me my ashplant (imagine following someone you don't know through nightown, there may have been things he'd like to try I suppose) and took me to the shelter. I can hear the way he said it holding my ashplant in his left hand, right hand in mine : 'I think you dropped something, Stephen'.

THE BELL JAR (1963)

It was not queer, just a sultry summer, that summer they buried Dignam, and I didn't know what I was doing outside that pub. I'm funny about burials. The idea of being buried makes me nauseous, and Dignam was all there was to read in the papers – god-lillied headlines staring out at us on every corner and at the musty, Guinness-smelling mouth of every subway. None of my business really but couldn't help wondering what it was like, being buried with mud up to your eyes.

Thought it must be the worst thing in the world.

Dublin is a trial enough. By eight in the morning the slaked, Liffey-wet freshness that somehow seeped in through the night dispersed like a tall tale told after a superfluous dram. Murky-green at the bottom of the upright alabasters, the hot streets fluttered in the sun, the trams sighed and gloated, and the sly, spindly drunks blew spite in my eyes and lies down my throat.

I kept hearing about Dignam all that day, in the papers and streets until I couldn't get him out of my mind. It was like the first time I saw Rudy. For weeks afterwards, his head – was it a head, can I call it that? – drifted up when I fried the offal at breakfast or saw the face of Lenehan, who was responsible for that Throwaway fracas yesterday, and soon it was like I was carrying Rudy on a string, like a big, limbless balloon smelling of lamb's wool.

I knew something was wrong that summer, because all I could think about was Dignam and how stupid I'd been to buy all those fashionable, expensive clothes for Molly, hanging pristine in her wardrobe like strips of saltfish, and how all the little triumphs of the well-placed ads fizzled to nothing now outside the red-bricked terraces and OPEN signs of Temple Bar.

I was supposed to be in the prime of my life.

I was supposed to be the envy of men all over Dublin who wanted nothing more than to walk in my size seven patent leather shoes as Mr Bloom out to lunch with a brown patent leather belt and brown patent leather pocket-book to match. And when my ads come out in a magazine the dozen of them in the Ormond – drinking whiskies with the skimpy, false hourglass barmaids, like shopdolls stuffed with sponge, on some Heavenly High, in the company of a group of young students with all-Irish cheekbones polished for the occasion – everyone would think I was having the time of my life.

Look what can happen in this country, they'd say. A Jew lives in some out-of-the-way place for over ten years, while we're so poor we can't afford a paper, and now he's with the Bard with his scholarship-winning prizes here and there, back in Dublin with his own private chaperone.

Only I wasn't chaperoning anyone, not even myself. I just jumped from the cemetery to lunch to the tower to the trolley-bus. I suppose I should have been excited by who they thought I was but I couldn't get myself to react. I felt very sad and very empty, the way the centre of Dignam's head must feel, lying still amidst the crumbling landmass of worms and surrounding hullabaloo.

GRAVITY'S RAINBOW (1973)

A seagull screams across the sky. This has happened before, but there is nothing to compare to it now.

Is it too late? As if the viceregal procession still proceeds, this is pure theatre. There are no lights inside the trams. No lights anywhere. Above them the girders of the docks old as a metallic king, and all this stone up high above the world that will not let the light of day through. But it's night. Bloom is afraid that the stone will fall – dumph! – and it will be a spectacle : the fall of a stone kingdom. But walking through Dublin in secret, without a glint of light, only their hearts beating.

Inside the pub, which is odd on several levels, they have nothing to smoke, their shoulders nearer and farther rub and connect, sweat expiring in puffs, a vibration in the frame of the carriage, a positioning, an unsettledness, all the others pressed in around, tired ones, black sheep, all out of luck and money : drunks, old sailors still in shock from their loss twenty years on, beggers in city clothes, derelicts, exhausted men with more children than it seems could belong to anyone, stacked about among the rest of the crowds to be couriered out to salvation. Only the nearer faces are visible at all, and at that only as pale-cindered discs in a penny-viewer, grogblossomed VIP faces behind cavalcade carriages cantering through the city ...

They have begun to move it seems. They pass on the lines, out of Sandymount Station, out of the West of Dublin, and begin pushing into more cramped, desolate parts of the city. Is this the right thing? Faces turn to the windows, but no one dares ask, not out loud. Rain comes down. No, this is an untangling and something he's been knitted into – they go in under archways, blacked-out entrances of rotted sandstone that look like bunkers in a sand dune ... certain rafts of blackened metal have moved slowly by to their left, and the smells of steam from days far to the past, smells of Dublin winters, of Sundays when no traffic came through, of the court cases and curious tourist growth, around the blind corners and the lonely avenues, a stifling smell of horse emissions, of maturing dung, dampening down the emptying streets rancid and deep, especially at dusk, with brown buttons closing their passageways, to try to bring the day's events to a climax ... and it is harder the deeper they go ... ruinous even to be secret in a city of such observant people, people whose *names he has never heard* ... the walls break down, the truths get fewer and so do the chances of light. The road, which was supposed to be opening out into a broader tramway, has instead been getting narrower, more broken, cornering tighter and tighter until all at once, almost too soon, they are under the final arch : brakes grab and squeal terribly. It is a Judgement from which there is no return.

THE HANDMAID'S TALE (1985)

I had slept in what had once been the defence tower. The floor was of galvanised stone, with sand and grit in it, for many feet had formerly trod there; the windows were still there though the lookers had long gone. A balcony ran around the tower, for the viewers, and I thought I could smell, faintly like an aftertaste, the pungent crust of seaweed, scored with the salt-tang of clawing crab and rosehip from the walking girls, petticoated as I knew from pictures, and in garters, exposed ankles, spoor-green seadew in their hair. Meetings would have been held there; the silence lingered, a numbness of unmade remarks, sigh upon sigh, an under-the-breath drollness, a forgotten want, signatures made on yellow paper by uncared-for maniacs, a stone orb of perspectives, powering the men with a shower of light.

There was no sex in the room and a strong need-for-it, an expectation, of something without form or name. I remember that feeling, for the thing always about to take place though never the same as the hand that touches us there, or wherever, in the back of the pub or the hidden lot, or the small room with the curtains drawn and only the pictures watching the revealing of flesh.

I wanted the future. How do I learn to make it, to satiate my talents? It was in the air and is still in the air, an aftertaste, as I tried to sleep, in the military bunks that have been set in rows, in separate rooms so we could not talk. We had starched sheets, like Victorians, and army-issue blankets, old ones that still said MARTELLO. I never folded my clothes neatly though resisted making stools at the end of the bed. The lights were dimmed but not turned out. Aunt Sara and the midwives, tied cauls attached to their leather belts.

No words though, they could not be trusted with words. Words are for the poets, those selected by the Seraphim. The poets weren't allowed in any administration except when called, and when they were they weren't allowed out, except after hours, walking alone around the fields which were hedged like prison grounds. The Seraphim stood outside earshot with their backs to us. They are objects of fear now, but of promise as well. If only they would look. If only I could talk to them. Something could be created, I think, some pact formed, some swap for their form and my body. This is a new kind of mythology.

I am learning to whisper almost without a sound. In sum-of-the-darkness I can stretch out my arms, when the others aren't looking, and touch the walls of the silent space. I'm learning to read my unwritten work, my head flat on the bar, turned sideways as if watching my own mouth. In this way my name is becoming imprinted in the stone and in the heavens.

Ste. Phen. De. Da. Lus.

FUGITIVE PIECES (1996)

Time is a one-legged sailor.

Blind sailor, tap-tapping the rim-tip on the cobbles of the darkened city. For nigh-on a thousand years the fish had slowly become drinkers at the gold taps of the old fountains. Cabmen's shelters built to watch the sun were flooded by the sleepless who walked the Liffey River. Gardens grew curious in suburban enviousness; lilacs, roses, bindweed.

No one is born a resident. If you're lucky, you'll leave an exile in someone's arms; or unlucky, wake up when your three score is done and face the terror of the last ten with brandy firing your skull.

He shrank from the crowd like a tolerant man, an aggrieved man, like a boy uprooted in the middle of O'Connell Street in the midst of a beer drought, five hundred drinkshocked heads like a ring of helmeted warriors. Dripping with the bog-stained phlegm of their room-temperature stout. Afterbirth of hops.

He saw a man spewing into his hat. He was heaving. His sudden politeness appalled him. For a minute he thought he would arrest him, or perhaps like the man of his own fantasy, dig a hole so deep he would then reappear in another part of the world.

THE ROAD (2006)

When he woke in the words and the dark and the cold of the night he'd reached out like a child into the air beside him. Night dark before darkness and the mornings more hot each one more than the one that had gone before. Like the onset of some bleak aria blackening out the world. His hand now rose and fell with each precious dreg. He pushed away the glass toby jug and raised himself in the stinking rose and smokiness and looked towards the east for any star there was none. In the dream he'd drank himself into he was in the cave shadows on the wall. Shadows of animals moving over the dark stone walls. Like a figure in a fable a swivelling host inside the innermost parts of the text's gigantic beast. Deep sapphire fires where the water dragged and stung. Tilling in the silence the minutiae of the air in which minutes and hours added to the year's surcease. Then he and Bloom stood in this small wooden room where lay the stout's black and ancient lake. And on the far shore of the bar a creature raised its dripping mouth from the glassrimmed pool and stared into the light with dead white eyes as blind as the barrels of soldiers. It swung its mouth low over the stout as if to smell the scent that it could not see. Sitting there pale and forked and luminescent, its bowels and bones cast up in the shadow on the bags of nuts and scratchings behind it. Its piles, its racing heart. It swung its head from side to side and then gave out a dry moan and lurched away limping soullessly into the dark.

With the first ring of the bell he rose and left Bloom sitting and walked out to the road and unbuttoning sighed and watched his own liquid flow to the south. Beaten, solemn, godless. He thought it was the seventeenth of June but he was unsure. He hadn't checked the time for hours. There'll be no surviving the rest of the year here.

When he was finished he buttoned himself and lifted his glass raising it to the houses below. Every dreg sliding back into his neck. The stiff ashplant swinging in loose swirls over the rooftops. He scolded what he could see. The serrated edges of terraces among the closing pubs. Looking for anything of promise. Any movement ...

A GIRL IS A HALF-FORMED THING (2013)

For her. She'll soon. I'll give her name. In the yellow of her skin she wears my name. Mother mine? Yes, me. Stitch the sheet. I said. I said that's what she said. She lay me down. They cut me from her. Wet and here and done.

Waking up in dormitories up the steps. Are you awake Stephen? Will you listen, he says. No. I want she I say. I want mother. Smell of rose from her skin. Petals pink and flaking fragrant. Scent of her in my eyes. Her pulse in my heart. Beating mum mum mum. At home she lives all around my room. Toolaroom, my mother's womb. Where she? Mother. What have I done? Mother. Green bile. Aftertaste burns. Rnnsssssss. Mother, all done. Out. She cried. Pray for me Stephen. No.

Sing I would. The wrong request. Liliata rutilantium. Naming. Rosepetals, bedsores. She no longer holds. Hold where you are. Plates and bedpans clatter, I hear them. You are young Stephen. Ruined by overthought. An egg, treacherous fry. Fall from heights. Can't hold. Or want to. Experience. Kicking in the cockles. Bang my. Wrists wrapped in vellum and texts bleed through. She felt the sick of her boy lost. Rnnsssssss.

She saw me first before I saw with my eyes. Parlour games : don't hold too long or the wind will change. I am not without mother. Feet stuck. A tishoo. Tishoo.

We all fall down.

You have found the man in black in D4.
Beyond a parked LEXUS a small brass plaque
reads THERAPIST.

How do you rate your man?s chances?

?I?d like to drop in on that discourse : eaves-
drop. Fly on the wall. Paddle in the pebbledash.
My ear fluttering on the picture rail. Moth.

Would you like to metempsychosise?
>Y GOTO 137
>N GOTO 162

CIRCE

*Act 4, Scene 5: Elsinore. A room in the castle /
A therapist's home in contemporary Dublin. Midnight.*

The therapist dimmed the lamp behind Stephen's head and sat silently out of view. A shadow of a man inside his mind. The therapist stroked back his tonsured hair : a Rolex flashed its quicksilver. In a far corner of the room, behind a tower of books, a moth peeled itself from the wallpaper. Flowers were strewn across the floor and across the surfaces, giving to the room a sap-like scent, mixed with decay.

– I want you to relax now Stephen and tell me how things have been for you since your mother's passing.

The voice, disembodied, held him in its timbre : a wave without summation. The smashed chandelier in the whorehouse crystallized in Stephen's mind : a constellation of glass around the wick of an ashplant.

– I am a broken chord in her universal music.

The moth hovered.

– What do you mean by that Stephen?

Its hindwings peeled then folded on a hinge back to its frame.

– I ... My mother has been appearing to me. I am being pursued by Hamlet.
– In dreams?
– Dreams that I can't wake from.

Stephen sensed the therapist smiling : a seesaw grin across his omnipotent mouth.

– Do these delusional states take place only when you're alone?
– As fact : yes. Agenbite of inwit. Yet if I can't see you, my mother is more real than you are. I both hear her voice and see her flesh. The Dane doubles me.
– The mind, Stephen, is a powerful thing. Not everything it shows has a hold in reality.
– Have we not moved on from Plato's cave? Can the animals of shadow not be pulled into the ark of understanding?
– That's why we're here Stephen. To work together on this.
– I said yesterday that my father is someone I've heard of. Today I am yet to hear from him.
– You feel, I sense, a lack of support through this difficult time?

– I am without a home.
– Can you not return?
– My father is a flawed herder of his daughters. The future of my sisters is tenuous.
– This must be a difficult time for your father?

Stephen hesitated : the vellum of his words puckered.

– This morning I saw my mother appear in my bedroom. A form without logic. Her face a white bedhanging, her features gone. She could not speak to me.
– If she could speak Stephen, what would she say?
– She'd tell me of the moocow.
– The moocow?
– A dream of what was. The slow hoofs of my nursery. Before the shaming of Parnell.
– What changed that?
– A boy called Nasty Roche.
– This was at school?
– Outside of school : the bonedamp mud of a national sport. Others watched.
– You were away from home at this time?
– Lovely mother was not there.
– Did you miss her?
– I returned at Christmas. Her eyes were wet. Aunt Dante had removed her purple brush for Parnell.

Silence. Stephen spoke first :

- Today I fell in love with a girl and saw the body of a dead man.
- The drowned man?
- I was second to the scene, I arrived as the sea spewed him out.
- What did you do?
- I vomited on his head.
- Is this another of your metaphors?
- Today I speak only in fact. My stomach was weak from excess.
- Is there something in this Stephen, this – instinctive recoil from death?
- Algy ... Swinburne ... said the sea is a great white mother. It is this endless nothing from my mother that is making me sick.
- Yet this was a man?
- He died a man. When he returned he had a woman's face.
- The face of your mother?
- Yes.

The therapist sighed. With hesitant halfassurance he spoke :

- Sometimes, Stephen, meeting our neurosis head-on like this can lead to resolution. It forces us to change our habits of thinking.
- I live by the sea. The tide comes in, the tide goes out. A dead man crests each wave.
- There is, Stephen, much life in the sea.

- All that lives must die, passing through nature to eternity.
- Eternity comes after death, but only after.
- Eternity is no good to me. I have a book to write.
- All writers have faced this. There is an argument that having to face the fact of death provides the inspiration for achievement on earth.
- This is the selfworthy pomp spouted by those who have only potboiled.
- If you don't want to die Stephen, but can't complete your work, what is it that you actually want?

Stephen sighed : exhalation without sibilants. The therapist waited. Through a break in the curtains a streetlamp stirred its oils along the side of a carriage. Hoof and halftone : the colliding stimuli of the poet. Stephen looked again : the carriage was a waxed black Lexus. The accumulation of the therapist's many listening hours. Stephen spoke :

- Your car moves less quickly across time than the novelist's words.
- There is an art to listening too Stephen, and my work necessitates travel.
- You pay for it with the wages of Dublin's parents?
- I pay for it with the wages I earn.
- I have no need of a Lexus to necessitate travel : my lexicon will take me back to Europe.
- What is it that you're running from Stephen?
- A doctor, an Englishman and a milkwoman.
- Must you always speak in such riddles?

– Synecdoches are my only clarity.
– You mentioned earlier, Stephen, that something happened today that you wished to discuss – A girl?
– Yes, I met a girl. The milkhag has transformed to a nymph.
– Who was she?
– She asked me about Yeats and had stitched boards for the women of Dun Emer Press. She praised my work.
– Will you see her again?
– I see her now. She wears nothing but white.
– What else was said?
– Words words words.
– You talked for long?
– All time takes place at once. We looked, talked, married, aged and were knitted as one package back into the earth.
– How, Stephen, does this girl differ from those you have been visiting in Monto?
– There are less creases beneath her frock.
– Interesting that you still define her by her body, as well as seeing her as Other. Perhaps you make an ideal of her?
– I am through with the Platonists of this city. She was no imagined form : I saw hairs on her arm where she brushed the rails. Her elbow was marked with a large brown mole.
– Are you Hamlet to this Ophelia?
– Do not mention him! He shadows me through Dublin. I am much relieved by his disappearance to England.

– You believe his love for Ophelia was not true? – Did he not jump into her grave?
– All copulation is a jump into a grave. We dust down the soil and make our excuses. By cock we are to blame.
– You have talked before of your long search for a woman like this, the games with Mercedes as a child, the pining through Dublin's streets. Is this, then, her ... the *one?*
– I feel different today than yesterday. Yesterday I had a winning horse and told no one. Today I have won a girl and must talk to a horse.
– You woke this morning seeing your mother's corpse Stephen, there is no therapist worth their salt who would not make this connection between her death and this girl in white.
– This is the observation of an ordered mind.
– You refuse to see it?
– What really am I able to see? My whole being is fatuous. My creator devised my first conception under the title *Stephen Hero* : what more apt metaphor for the burning of the wings of ambition?
– He did this perhaps from love, to give you the fullest chance of becoming?
– He did this to polish the wingmirror of his art into a more oblique reflection of my face. In *Hero* I had features, whole pages were spent in description of my hair. I remember the line: 'A girl might or might not have called him handsome.' My mouth feminine. His portrait of me was nothing but a fluffer for onanistic aesthetes : I have become lost behind the language.

> Like a film left in the sun : I fade towards transparency.

– You don't feel his love, that he wanted you to be the best you could be?
– He burned my first incarnation, only half of the thousand pages survived the flames.
– Perhaps this was to give you the best chance to fully become yourself?
– His sister saved me. I owe more to her than him.
– He penned you.
– And threw me. Sometime I feel like the vacuous container for his late night debauchery.
– I refer you, Stephen, to what he said to Nora.
– Ah, her. He forced me to watch them have sex.

The therapist picked up a book and began to read :

– 'Now, my darling Nora, I want you to read over and over all I have written to you. Some of it is ugly, obscene and bestial, some of it is pure and holy and spiritual; all of it is myself.'
– Yes, himself. Where am I in it?

THERAPIST : What, Stephen, do you think you might gain from questioning your conception like this?
STEPHEN : I have two mothers. Both are dead. The first was a man called James : he liked to watch women urinate.
THERAPIST : It is interesting that you see Mr Joyce as a mother and not a father.

STEPHEN : Bloom's feminineness flowed from the author's anima. He loved women because he was so in touch with the one inside himself.

THERAPIN : There is nothing to be scared about in being sensitive to our feminine aspects.

STEPHENIST : Tell me more.

THERAPIN : Once, as a girl, a boy felt under my petticoats and recoiled from what he found there.

STEPHENIST : What was there?

THERAPIN : A partick thistle. I was too confused to tell anyone.

STEPHENIST (singing) :
She is dead and gone, lady,
She is dead and gone;
At her head a grass-green turf,
At her heels a stone.

In the blind dark corner the therapist blew his cockling nose into the rag of the past. He took out a paper bag from which he plucked flowers and herbs and began to throw them on the ground in front of him, like a clown at his own funeral. Tufts of rosemary, wax-seals of pansies, sprigs of fennel, fresh daisies and violets. Between each handful of thrown leaves he wiped his nose on a handkerchief.

STEPHENIST : There, there. 'Once upon a time and a very good time it was there was a moocow coming down along the road and this moocow that was coming down along the road met a nicens little boy named baby tuckoo.'

THERAPIN : Stephen?
STEPHENIST : Yes.
THERAPIN : Could you give me a hug?
STEPHENIST : Yes, but where are you?
THERAPIN : I'm here in the corner, next to the self-help books.

Stephen turned. Voice without matter. The ineluctable modality of the visible was a mistake.

The voice alone was ineluctable.

```
This platform is no longer supported.
>GOTO 165
```

MAPS : PART II

Another part of the platform / 7 Eccles Street　　　*151*

A room in Polonius' House / Eccles Street,
　to Sir John Rogerson's Quay　　　*152*

A room in the castle / Glasnevin cemetery　　　*153*

A room in the castle / Inside Bloom's head　　　*154*

A hall in the castle / Ormond Quay　　　*155*

A room in the castle / a brothel in Monto　　　*156*

The Queen's closet / Central Dublin
　1904 and 2014　　　*157*

A room in the castle / Temple Bar　　　*158*

Another room in the castle /
　Barney Kiernan's pub　　　*159*

Another room in the castle /
　Sandymount Strand　　　*160*

A plain in Denmark / the Martello Tower　　　*161*

Elsinore. A room in the castle / Dublin 4　　　*162*

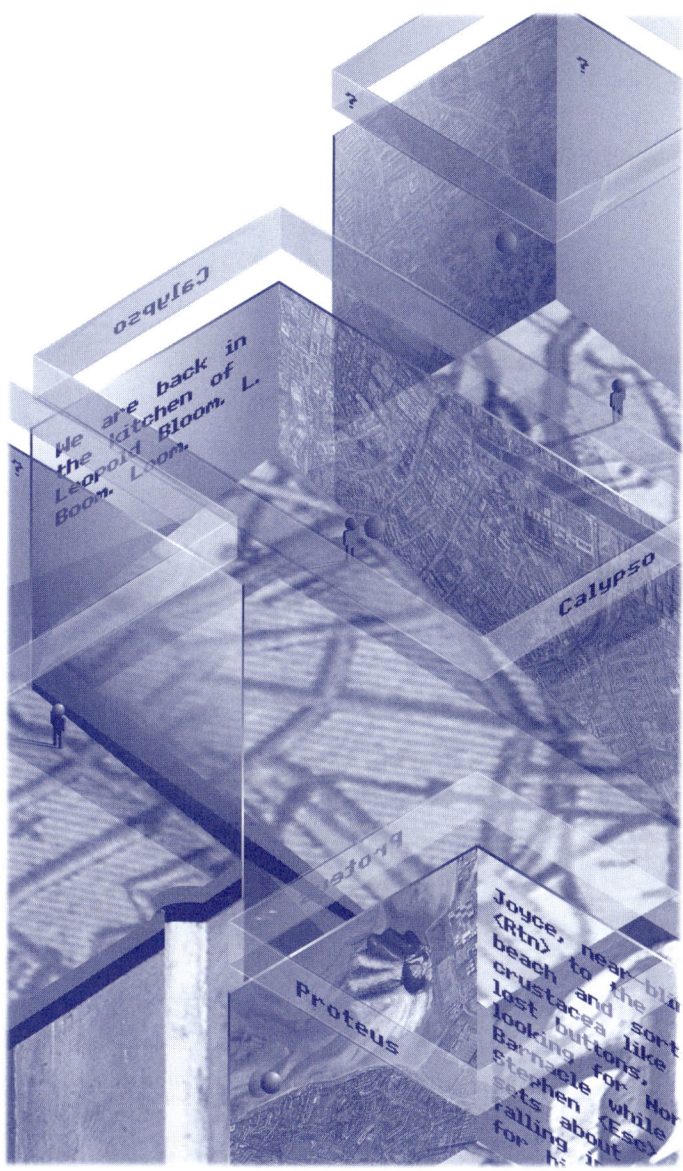

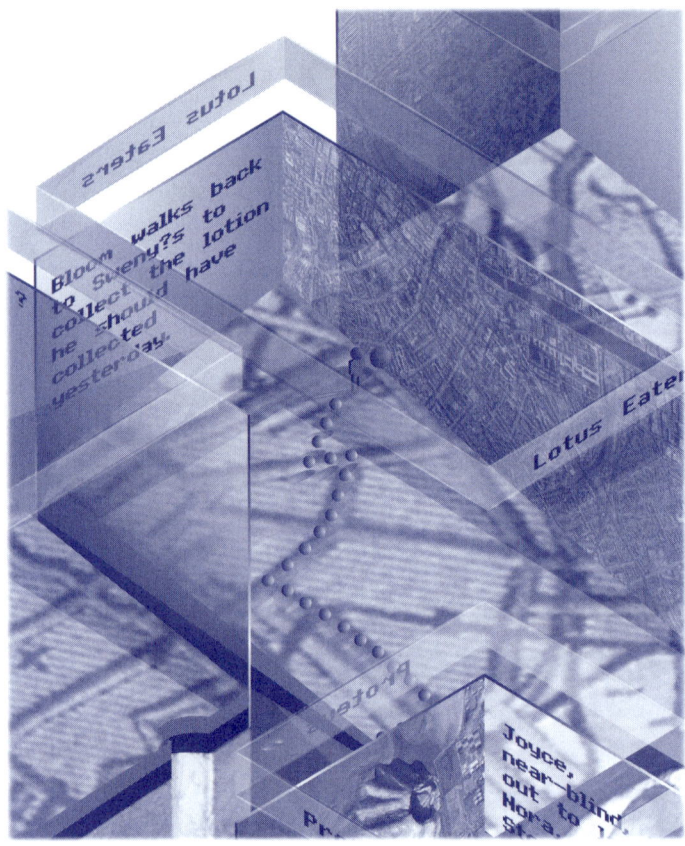

```
You are on a platform before a castle. A Per-
spex sign says MUSEUM. A sign reads CLOSED.

?Give the door a good hard push

You try and push the door but pass through in-
stead, stumbling into a ticket office. There is a
bottle marked POISON and a COOKIE on the table.

?Accept the cookie
>GOTO 225

?Pick up the bottle
>GOTO 51
```

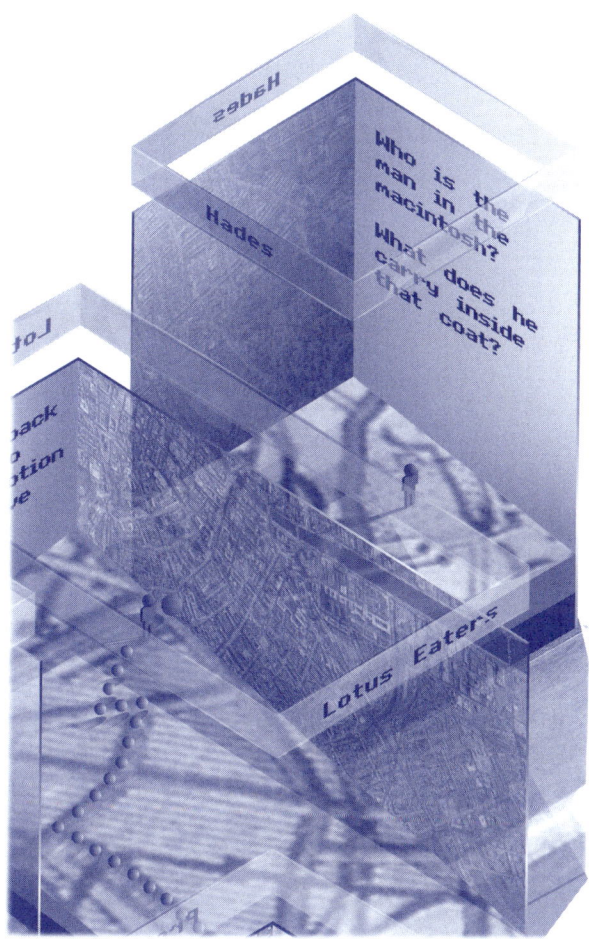

Your hand passes through the bottle. Through a partition you see a man in black, followed by two men in mackintoshes.

?O. No. Am I? Passed over? Deceased???!!!
>GOTO 226

?Enter player 2 : L. BOOM
>GOTO 59

```
You approach a glass vitrine. A sign :
EXHIBIT REMOVED FOR CLEANING.

?Follow the man in black. Face like
Molly. Or like Rudy would?
>GOTO 227

?Follow the men in mackintoshes! Gardai.
Must report myself dead. Murdered, even!
>GOTO 67
```

You are in a cafe in a hall of the castle. You hear the espresso machine dial-up a cappucino.

?I?m dead hungry.
>GOTO 228

?Where has that man in black got to?
>GOTO 71

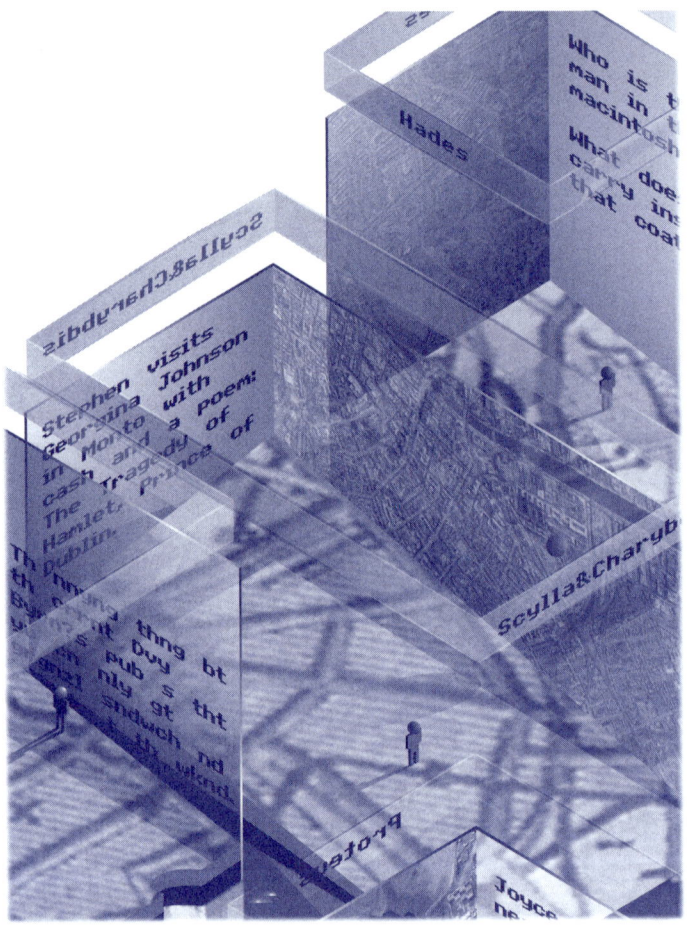

```
You enter another room in the castle.
QUEEN GERTRUDE and KING CLAUDIUS are here,
holding hands. Laughing and carousing.

?Queen Gertrude my hat! That?s Molly and Boylan!
>GOTO 229

?Something is rotten in the state of Dublin.
>GOTO 79
```

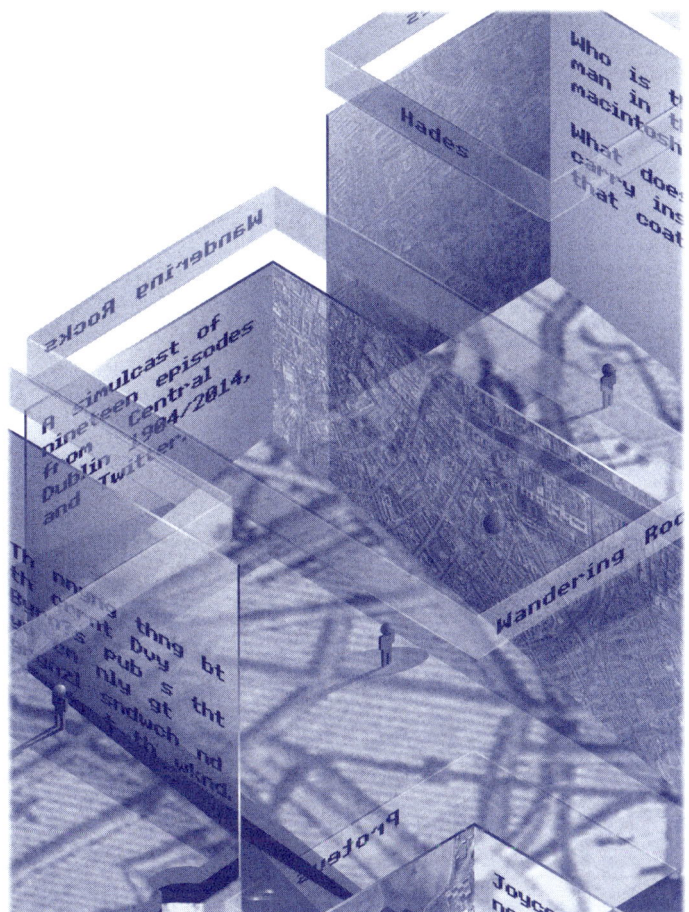

QUEEN GERTRUDE and KING CLAUDIUS enter her closet. So the WHOLE EAR OF DUBLIN is rankly abused.

?Follow them. No wait : BLOCKBLOCKMUTEMUTE!!!
>GOTO 230

?A serpent stung me! Noble youth /The serpent that did sting thy father?s life /Now wears his crown :-(
>GOTO 87

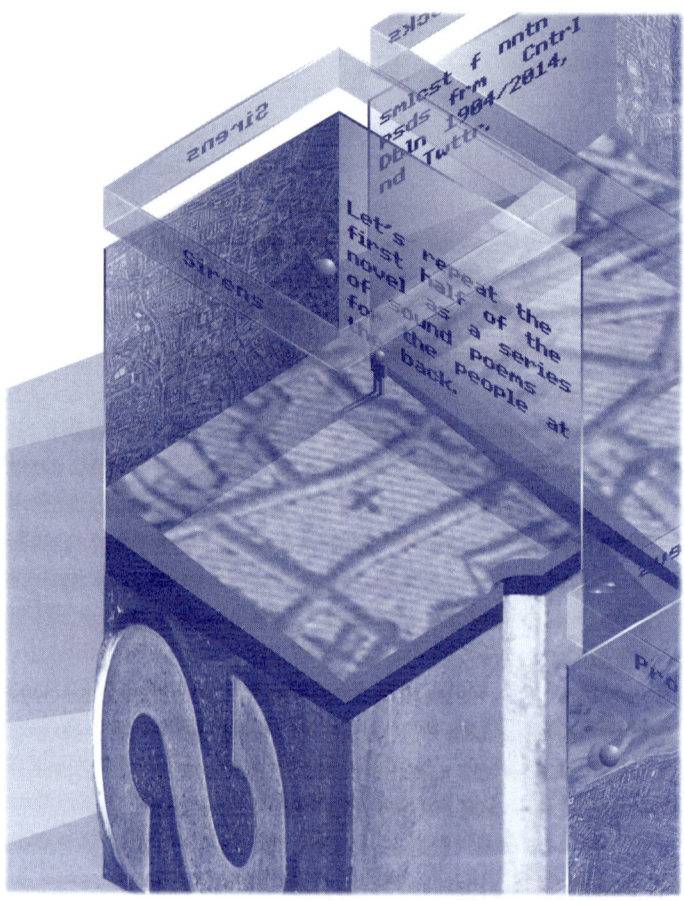

```
You enter another room in the castle, next door
to QUEEN GERTRUDE?s closet.

?god aren?t I just reduced to a breeze.
<Esc>.
>GOTO 159

?What brought us to this? Dash some objects
against their wall. Add my supernatural groans
to their unnatural ones. Plug my ears with wax!
>GOTO 231
```

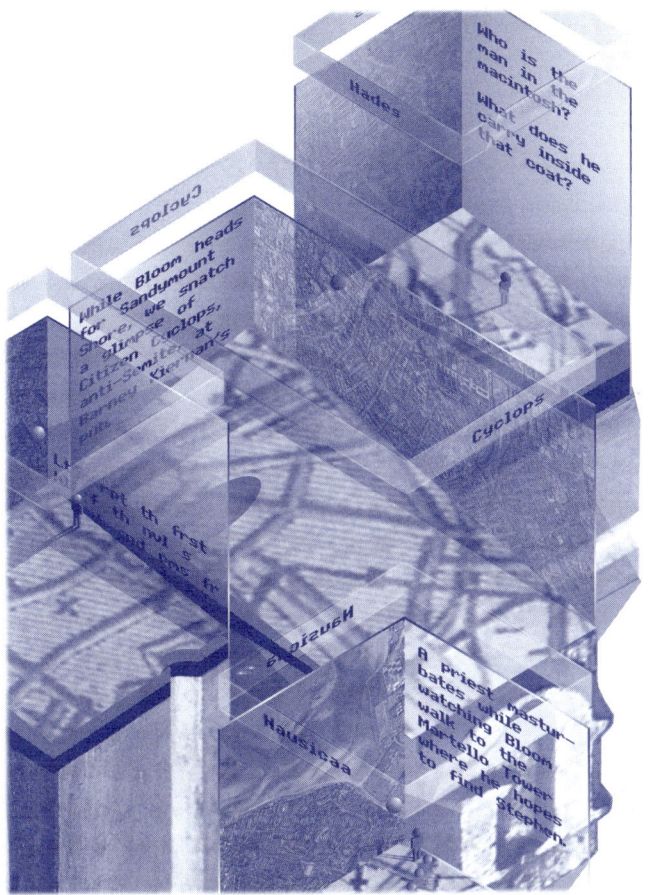

The men in mackintoshes enter your room with an ENVELOPE. They talk, unaware of your presence. They are CLAUDIUS?s libel lawyers, ROSENCRANTZ & GUILDENSTERN. The ENVELOPE contains a very harsh review, by CLAUDIUS, of a book written by the man in black.

?I must find and warn that youth in black.
>GOTO 160

?Revenge my FOUL and most unnatural murder!
>GOTO 232

```
You enter another room in the castle.
There is a stage. Servants are unfolding
chairs. A playbill reads : ULYSSES.

?Find the man in black : a poet! We might
adapt this ULYSSES to suit both our purposes!
>GOTO 234

?Find the script to this ULYSSES. This polter-
geist will insert a bit to boil Boylan?s blood.
Molly, my widow, will weep for me yet.
>REPEAT
>GOTO 95
```

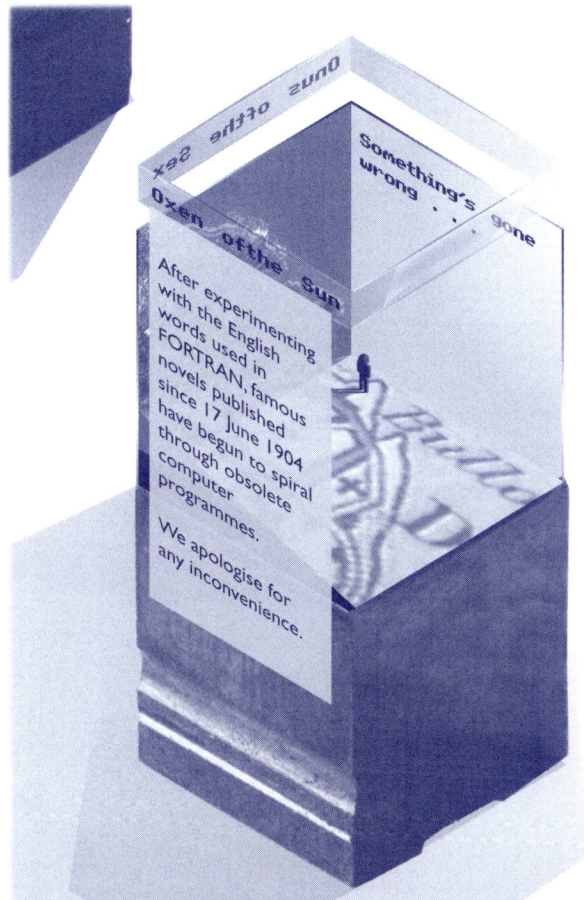

```
You appear on a windswept plain. The castle is
in the distance. The man in black has been here.

?Goto nighttown. We?ll find him bowling from gut-
ter to gutter like a ten-pin ball at a Leisure-
plex kids party.
>GOTO 235

?Goto the Martello Tower. We?ll find him throwing
a stick for denouement : a sea-wet dog.
>GOTO 119
```

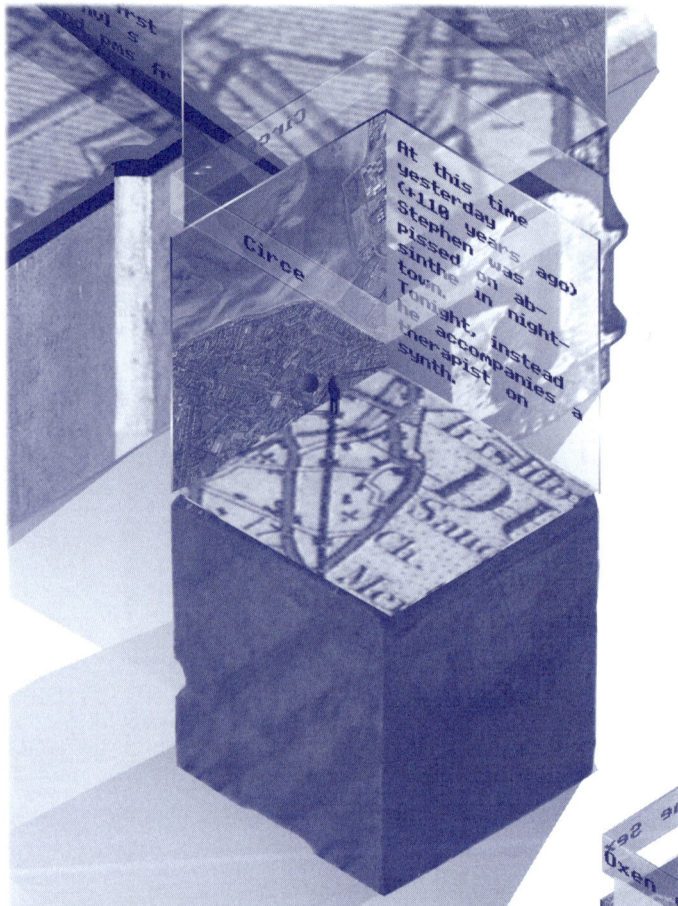

CONGRATULATIONS! You have survived!
You appear in yet another room in the
castle : the man in black lays on a
couch.

?Isn?t it always the last place you look.
Wait, that?s DEDALUS! Just the man for
the job!

>Hi-SCORE. PLEASE ENTER YOUR NAME
>GOTO 236

Part III

EUMAEUS

*Act 4, Scene 6: Another room in the castle /
A carriage travelling to St. Stephen's Green. 1am.*

The station rafters reminded Bloom of skeletal remains he'd seen in a book. A dinosaur or gargantuan seacreature. The ribs of the structure had blackened into a geometry of crosshatched lines.

    Leaving Westland Row Station Stephen moved with purpose past the Doric arch of St George's Church, the opened hands of the statuette God looked down with a questioning frown. Tufts of wildgrass bowed in clumps over the edge. In dropshadowed gold the Latin read : DEO OPTIMO MAXIMO SUB INVOC B ANDREÆ APOSTOLI. Light spilt in golden cups across the wet pavements as Stephen walked towards the brown glass plated doors of Kennedy's bar. The door stuck firm on its latch. Stephen placed his ashplant against the wall and looked with jeweller's nighvision to the bar inside. Damn it he thought, they drink without me.

    Bloom peered past the young man's shoulder : Sweny, the pharmacist, stood at the centre of a pack of latenight revellers. The barman looked back to the two men and cut his throat with the mockblade of his hand signifying with sound and fury that last orders had passed. Barabbas, Stephen muttered.

A horse moved towards them in sad hollowsounding clops. Bloom signalled the jarvey and the two men clawed themselves up into the hackney cab. The jarvey straightened in his seat : business. He tightened the slack reigns around the sleeping horses. Bloom spoke :

– Drive around a little please, then to St. Stephen's Green.
– That, whispered Stephen : was mine.

The jarvey gave out a fierce *Yah* and the carriage began to move. Stephen fell back on the leather couch as Bloom rose upright into the seat. He coughed into his hand. Stephen spoke first :

– Newton's first law of his *Principia Mathematica* : my body is an object that cannot stay constant when acted on by force.

Bloom's body bristled the darkness excitedly :

– The laws of classical mechanics. I wish I could have read it in the original Latin.
– *Cave quid volunt.*
– Latin I never learnt. I showed you the Hebrew last night, remember?

Stephen looked sideways crossly at Bloom.

– What is it you want with me Leonard?
– You continue to call me Leonard.
– And?
– My name is Leopold. Leopold Bloom.
– I taught a class on naming this morning. There's nothing you can teach me.
– I. I don't – want, anything.
– You took me home last night. This afternoon you turned up at my prison.
– My wife, you remember the photo?

Bloom reached for his pocket as the jarvey spoke :

– By Gob these roads are chaos Sir I swear his High Squire's cavalcade set me back three shillings at least yesterday ...
– Yes.

Bloom turned to speak to the distancing Stephen ...

Chaos, the jarvey said, pushing his fraught head to the side and shouting across to a passing cab :

– Don't pass down that way, the road's tighter than a Jew's grip!

In Bloom's hand the wellthumbed picture of Molly-in-bloom sat perched for Stephen's attention.

– I showed you last night, my wife –
– Yes, said Stephen.

The jarvey intervened :

– Let me tell you both ...

His unwashed head peered backways into the exposed cabin of the travellers :

– They pawn things in the pawnshop, you know, at Brereton's on Capel Street, and by Gob it's no rubbish let me tell you. Gold, mostly. And bronze.

The hoofirons of the horse clotted the rhythm of the rattling cart. They moved in syncopated trots towards the docks. Along the lightlittered surface of the water a child's wooden boat bobbed. Its lone owner, somewhere, must be sleeping. Further along, against the gingerbread backdrop of a warehouse, a man and a woman were kissing.

The carriage passed the twin turrets of Boland's Flour Mills at Grand Union Dock. The arrangement of small illmatching windows poured out steam. Bloom counted them, headturned, as they passed : ten, twenty, thirty, thirty-five, forty, forty-two. Must be like Hades in there today, phew, devil's business. Someone should limit their working hours. Age too. No sooner popped out than handed over. Blackened faces, hands like coalminers. No protection see.

Stephen spoke :

– Your wife I know, I've seen her while I've been about the streets, at my art –

– Your art! The jarvey shouted. Let me tell you about one man I know and his art. This man, let's call him Nobodaddy, I heard he took the whole of his wife's jewellery box to Brereton's, worth a hundred shillings if a penny. The pawnbroker offered back twenty. I can tell you both now there is a jew in jewellery. The man moved him up to forty. There was a deal to be struck there, at least enough to see him through the lean times – by Gob, there's enough of those ...

Stephen and Bloom let the mistrustful silence envelop the shared carcass of the carriage. They were on John Rogerson's Quay, the Liffey widened around them in a welter of ripple and undertow. The Custom House, lit with electric light, seemed to lure them forward with promises of overseas rewards : emeralds, orangeblossom, tea. Bloom spoke :

– You were saying, my wife you've seen?
– There was an artwork too you see, shouted the jarvey, along with the jewels ...

The man's voice hauled its net over them :

– An artwork, lovely drawing it was. The size of – see that window over there? – The size of that, to be hung on a wall see. It was all the man had left in the world, even his feet were covered with buckskin. *Bunny* they called him, his ears twitched like rabbits' you see. His hard times had untold depths : his wife, eating less than him, had had an affair with another man you see. Yet it was *him* that had to feed *her*. Poor sod. The painting had been on the wall when they'd moved into the house. He had hoped, at most, that it might be worth five shillings, enough for a last pot of stew and a week from the bailiffs. He took it in, laid it down on the desk and said nothing : he knew, you see, that it was best to wait for the offer than to say something ...

The jarvey ducked : a seagull crawed, skimming its brown underside against his tophat.

– Parasites, worse than rats they are! See them off the bridge attacking people, I blame those who feed them. It's only them that keeps the seedcake stall in business. Encourages them it does. By Gob and when people in this city are starving too ...
– The birds, said Bloom, need sustenance too. A bird can be fed on crumbs, at no expense.
– Sense? There is no sense, you're right Sir. Where was I? The painting, yes. The jew looked at it for five minutes, stroking his chin, then disappeared into the back of the shop. Out he came again, looked around, then disappeared. On his third appearance he said : *I will give you five pounds for this.* The man looked. He lifted the painting from the desk and made to leave the shop. The jew shouted after him, *Hold on! Make it ten!* Cash, on the spot. The man walked back, took the money and walked from the shop in the opposite direction to his house. Liverpool I heard is where he is now ...

From the window of the cab a policeman on a cycle pedalled pellmell alongside them. They passed the corner of Baggot Street.

Stephen spoke :

– The policeman of this city have impeccable shoes. I would like to see them in action.
– He has missed his target, Bloom said.

Two drunken men were walking, linked arm-in-arm, their bodies sledging through the night's liquid leak of gravity. Bloom went to speak, stopped : exhaled. Stephen spoke :

– My father does not understand the distinction between ante- and post-meridian. His clock cycles but once each day.
– A fine voice your father has Stephen, the way he suffers now won't be forever.
– A purgatorio of the mind can become an eternal state. He inflames it with brandy. All of his companions have fallen too. He blames Mulligan for my downfall : I only follow the course set down by bloodline.
– About my wife, Stephen, given that you asked. I wanted –

The jarvey turned and spoke, the sockets of his eyes pronounced with shadow :

– There she was Sir, the wife, right in position first thing this morning, nothing better, and worth the risk despite the seven children ...

Bloom snapped :

– Perhaps you could keep your private life to yourself! I am talking to my young friend here. If memory serves me correctly you are being paid to drive us to Stephen's Green : we don't require any extra services.

The jarvey withdrew : rain ran slick down his cloaked shoulders.

– As you will Sir ...

The carriage turned towards Trinity College passing an orchard of hollow warehouses. Many without windows except for thin rectangular slits high-up in the adobe walls. They trotted along on the calculus of the wet cobbles stopping briefly at the corner alongside O'Brien's pub. Festoons of summer flowers burst from the hanging baskets. Stephen peered from the window : a man, a messenger in the dress of a sailor, raised his hand to the window and handed Stephen a letter.

Bloom looked at Stephen and Stephen calmly shrugged as if to say there was nothing that could be presented to him that day that could possibly give him any more cause for alarm than finding a dead man on a beach. Bloom watched as he tore the yellow pages of the paper and read. When he was finished he folded the paper into his pocket and looked out of the window.

– I need to urinate.
– Could you not wait until Stephen's Green, we're turning towards there now? What did the letter say?

Stephen's folded hands whitened on the crook of the ashplant :

– I am not the God of my own anatomy.
– What was it the letter said Stephen? It wasn't by any chance intended for myself.
– That it was not. It was intended for me. He's back from England.
– Who is?
– The Dane.

The carriage turned left at the Royal College of Surgeons.

– The dwelling place of my own executioner, Stephen said.
– Who's that? asked Bloom.
– My landlord and tenant : Malachi Mulligan.
– Perhaps your father is right and he's leading you astray? I saw him heading for the train with Haines last night, with no regard for your wellbeing. Who is back from England, did you mean Haines, the Englishman?

– I am being pursued by a fictional Prince. Mulligan was already caustic because I had not met him at The Ship. I'd lent him money too, and bought him absinthe : this was my mistake, he took it with a medical coldness and without the artist's flair. He is more English than the Englishman : this is why the two of them dine together. They have made a shared mother of the milkwoman.
– Where will you sleep tonight?
– Somewhere green. The sickbowl of the city.
– You would be welcome back at my house. We have a spare bed, my daughter is away you see. I wanted to ask, about my wife –
– Stephen's Green! the jarvey hailed. Where would you like?
– Excuse me Stephen, Bloom blushed. Let me pay.

His plump dark hand plummeted into his pocket and pulled out a soft cradle of brown and gold coins. The jarvey took payment with a grunt and turned back to the steaming flanks of the horses. Stephen descended from the carriage first, oblivious to the hovering hand of Bloom. He spoke quietly to himself :

– Stephen's Green : I flew a kite here as a boy. Now I smell the corpserot of experience.

Behind them the carriage clattered in ironwet hooftrots. Its shadow disappearing behind the Royal College of Surgeons. Bloom turned to speak to Stephen :

– My wife, you see, I wanted to ask –

Where Stephen had stood was a small black puddle. Bloom's shadow fattened in slats through the rails. A dunnock or rat spasmed into the shape of a leaf. The trees were seeded with the scent of summer rain.

Through the lightslatted railings the statue of Robert Emmet, green and birdfouled, raised its boyish shoulders to the Georgian terraces of York Street. His veined hands clenched towards a fist. From the other arm a net of web strung inwards, attached to his leg. A transparent hindwing. The look of a dreamer, the body of a runner. The permanent impetuousness of youth.

A folded piece of paper sailed across the surface. Bloom stooped and picked it up :

St. Stephen's Green Traffic Management Scheme

In early September Dublin City Council announced a new traffic scheme that will make travelling in the St. Stephen's Green area easier and result in less disruption when the utility works for Luas Cross City begin in 2014. The council began work on the St. Stephen's Green Traffic Management Scheme on 9th September and is happy to announce that the first of two new right turns at St. Stephen's Green will come into effect on 21st November. This right hand turn will be from St. Stephen's Green South to St. Stephen's Green West to facilitate access to car parks in the area, particularly at York – Mercer's Street junction.

Click here to read the full press release.

www.dublincity.ie

BLOOM: Why are we stopping here?
STEPHEN: The performance is about to begin –

Act 4, Scene 7: Another room in the castle / the dressing-room of Sarah Bernhardt

SARAH BERNHARDT LIES IN A COFFIN, PREPARING TO RESURRECT HER PERFORMANCE OF *HAMLET* AFTER THE THEATRE SUCCESSES OF 1899 AND THE FILM OF 1900.

THE 'DIVINE SARAH' – BRILLIANT AND INDOMITABLE – IN HER PERFORMANCE AS HAMLET IN *DEDALUS*, A TALE OF TWO MEN SHADOWED BY A THIRD

... I ... Understand death from this, my bed. I must drowse in the eternal linen of the tragic ... A worthwhile commission. If I dream can I be him? A bed trick of guilt. If I sleep? I dream his death ...

A DIRECTOR APPEARS. WHITE-HAIRED, BEYOND MIDDLE-AGE, HE STOOPS OVER HER AND WHISPERS SOMETHING IN HER EAR. SHE OPENS HER EYES. HE TALKS FOR A MINUTE THEN LEAVES.

... The commission changes ... I must play a scene on a beach ... digging my own grave. A new Hamlet : the suicide is knitted in prose. I must excise subtlety and speed : four hours this lasts ...

... I must sleep, feel what it is to disappear in self-annihilation ...

> THE DIRECTOR REAPPEARS. THIS TIME WEARING A RED PAPER CHRISTMAS HAT. HE WHISPERS. HER EYES OPEN.

... A new rôle : the ghost of the mother of Hamlet's double ... a contemporary figure of the tragic ... do I appear in guilt? No, the guilt is his. White is the colour for that, streaked in sand-brown stains ...

> THE DIRECTOR REAPPEARS, STILL WEARING THE HAT AND SMOKING A CIGAR. SHE OPENS HER EYES AS HE TALKS. HE DISAPPEARS. FAR OFF, A BABY STARTS TO CRY.

... The other Hamlet is a real person, Dedalus his name is. His grief needs no enactment. This is the New Theatre. This is why I sleep in this coffin. When my eyes open tomorrow the first Act begins. My controversy is propelled by my sex. Can I give the play its much needed bedtrick? Introduce a cross-dress scene in place of the sea-change? The modern has arrived ... They must know I am the Divine Sarah. My *Hamlet* performances have rekindled the nerve-endings in Shakespeare's cheeks. If this novel is to define a period I must be in it. I must play that Hamlet. A new scene, set on the beach : I will dig my way into history ...

> THE DIRECTOR REAPPEARS, STILL WEARING THE HAT AND SMOKING THE PIPE. THE BABY HAS STOPPED CRYING; THE DIRECTOR NOW WALKS A DOBERMANN DOG WITH A CRYSTAL STUDDED COLLAR. SARAH LISTENS, EYES OPEN, A SLOW REACTION OF DISPLEASURE SPREADS ACROSS HER FACE. THE DIRECTOR DISAPPEARS AND LAERTES APPEARS.

DIVINE SARAH: The last time we met we duelled.
LAERTES: You stole the show from me.
DIVINE SARAH: What news this time?
LAERTES: A letter from Hamlet.
DIVINE SARAH: The real Hamlet – the one I will play?
LAERTES: There is someone else angling for this rôle.
DIVINE SARAH: Is he once more set naked on the kingdom?
LAERTES: No, he says he's watching a man look for library slips.
DIVINE SARAH: Is this some kind of joke?
LAERTES: More of a modern adaptation.
DIVINE SARAH: I will not downplay to the diurnal. The New Theatre requires gravitas.
LAERTES: He is not the hero of this book. The hero is a poet called Stephen Dedalus.

DIVINE SARAH: I will meet him on equal terms upon the beach.

LAERTES: I'm lost in it my lord. But let him come.

DIVINE SARAH: I shall overshadow this Stephen Dedalus! ... I can play no second fiddle, least of all to a contemporary and never to a man ... I will per form extempore and he can do the same : join me in sublime art. Thespian; from Thespis of Icaria : a poet ... I foresee in this scene that the inventor of characters plays out his ideas next to a man yet to find himself. I will occupy that. Will this Dedalus play himself?

SARAH BERNHARDT SITS UPRIGHT AND RINGS A BELL. THE DIRECTOR'S HEAD APPEARS. SHE WAVES HIM FORWARD AND TALKS IN HIS EAR. SHE WAITS FOR A RESPONSE. HE TALKS BACK TO HER.

... This character plays a younger version of the novel's author. A fictionalisation of who he might have been. My Hamlet is the one I am yet to become ... Will he meet me halfway in performance?

SHE SITS UPRIGHT ON THE BED.

DIVINE SARAH: Take me to the scene. I am ready.

ITHACA

Act 5, Scene 1: A churchyard / The mind of Chris McCabe.

When did you first read *Ulysses*?
1995, in the summer between finishing A-levels and the start of a degree in English Literary Studies at the University of Central Lancashire in Preston. I was seventeen years old.

Why then?
A commitment to literature. Regardless of my pending exam results I was *in* for literature for the long term. There was also a sense of outdoing my dad. One Sunday evening, drunk, at about 6.30pm, he had walked into my bedroom with his copy of the *The Essential James Joyce* and, sitting next to me on the bed, read out loud Joyce's poem 'Ecce Puer'. He had stopped to point out the personal significance of each line, for example : 'Of the dark past / A child is born', after which he commented : 'I guess that's *me*'. The ending in which the son pleads for forgiveness from the father was mortifyingly pertinent to him, after losing his dad ten years before. I was mortifyingly embarrassed by the whole episode.

Why mortifyingly pertinent? Why mortifyingly embarrassed?

Pertinent because his father's death had triggered the onset of a midlife crisis and alcoholism. *Embarrassed* because he was sitting on my bed : a personal space for reading, fantasy and masturbation. *Mortifyingly* because death was behind the whole episode. Looking back I can see that I was aware of my father's death long before his death was a twinkle in the undertaker's eye.

Was he ill?

Not at all, I might describe his state at that time as one of rude health. He was no doubt turning to alcohol as a form of self-medication to deal with his father's death and was drinking the best part of a bottle of vodka each evening; though his body was tolerant and would not, in fact, yield to the copious amount of spirits he drank in his lifetime.

How, then, did he die?

A glioma in the front left side of the brain, specifically glioblastoma multiforme, nine years after the incident in my bedroom.

Had he read *Ulysses?*

No.

Was his life the worse for it?

Not in any substantive way, though the hours put into drinking hard spirits might have been more fruitfully spent reading the book.

How so?
Engagement with characters with whom he might have felt affinities and questioned in fruitful ways. Engagement with Stephen for his fraught intellectual qualities and his pain, for his Jesuitical upbringing. My dad had his own painful memories of a Jesuit teacher who would make the children bang their chest with a fist while chanting *mea culpa, mea culpa, mea máxima culpa*. He would have liked Bloom for his lostness, his own grieving for his father's death. For his out-about-town inquisitiveness. He would have questioned Stephen's labouring pomposity. His verbosity. He would have questioned Bloom's tolerance of Boylan's invasion.

What books was he reading instead?
The *Colditz* series was a constant on his bedside table. As was *Catch-22* (unfinished).

I get the sense you'd rather not be questioned about your dead father?
Not at all, it's just that I wasn't expecting it.

Not even given the strong theme of fathers and sons in *Ulysses*?
There is a strong theme of adultery too, and of poetic aspiration : the questions might just have well been aimed in those directions.

What else was on your father's bedside table?
An ashtray. Stickers I'd taken from a box of *Sugar Puffs* when I was six years old and placed onto the MDF with-

out his permission. One said *I love you Dad*. Another said *Big Daddy*. A lamp. Beneath the table was a small cupboard which held old slippers and shoes.

Were any shoes missing?
Possibly. My dad always arrived into and left the house in a scramble. If your question is driving towards the death of Paddy Dignam and his missing shoe in *Ulysses*, and his later appearance via séance to say where the lost shoe is hidden, then I can say now that there is no point pursuing this line of questioning : my dad has not appeared to me since dying and lost shoes are the least of my concerns. Or his.

What was your father's profession?
For the largest part of his life he was an assistant manager of an office division within Girobank. Before that he worked in a furniture showroom and fitted carpets in people's homes. He became medically retired due to arthritis and then later took voluntary work driving people with cancer to receive treatment in Merseyside hospitals.

Is there an irony in him performing this work up until his own death via cancer?
In fact not. He had ceased that work shortly before his first illness of diabetes to become a cab driver. It was a line of work he despised. He had his first epileptic fit at the wheel of his cab in the rank outside the Asda in Huyton Village. Another driver described him slumped over the wheel as the cab rolled forwards of its own accord. He did receive treatment in a number of hospitals he had

driven patients to, including Whiston and Clatterbridge, this could be described as ironic, though I would prefer the word *unfortunate*.

What were his final words?
Unknown. His final words were a look. His look said more than words.

After such long immersion in *Ulysses* how can you be content to rest on a stock phrase such as 'his look said more than words'?
Indolence. A sense of fittingness. Refusal to dig deeper into what my father *not* having final words might mean. There is an unnoticed poetic depth to the phrase 'his final words were a look' which you have overlooked. This section will remain through the editing process.

That's what you think.
Are we done?

What else might he have actually read from *The Essential James Joyce*?
It's easier to say what he hadn't read. Not *Finnegans Wake*. Not *Exiles*. He had possibly read *A Portrait of the Artist*. Certainly *Dubliners*. Without question the poems.

Who was his favourite living writer?
He had none.

He had none?

He liked people who had been writers but by then they were all dead.

And of those dead writers?
Eric Arthur Blair.

Why not use the known name George Orwell?
My dad had played the same trick on me in September 1995. He was helping me move into my room in the halls of residence and after carrying up my clothes and placing my books on the shelf he filled my sink with cold water and submerged four cans of Kronenbourg into the water. The four cans bobbed in the Armitage Shanks sink. He said, as he put the books onto the shelf : 'My favourite writer is Eric Arthur Blair' to which I said 'I've never heard of him'. He then said: 'That was George Orwell's real name'.

So even as you outdid his learning through the taking of a degree he was also keen to assert his intellectual authority?
Icarus followed Daedalus. Joyce recycled his own father's phrase 'like a shot off a shovel', placing it in the mouth of Simon Dedalus. Stephen argues that the son and the father are incompatible because the son grows strong on the weakening of the father. When Stephen is asked in the cabman's shelter if he knows Simon Dedalus he responds, 'I've heard of him'.

What was your father's favourite Orwell book?
He'd read them all. He talked a lot about *Down and Out in Paris and London*.

Which of Orwell's novels had you read at that point in your life?
Animal Farm. The Road to Wigan Pier. Down and Out in Paris and London.

1984?
This was 1995.

Had you read *1984*?
I was yet to read it. I read it in 1996.

What was it you got from Joyce that wasn't in Blair?
Unexpectedness. Flair. Difficulty. Challenge. Compact imagery. Metrical patterning inside the prose. A window of frosted language through which character and narrative appear in oblique relation to the reader. Life and art coalescing : the life more real for the artistic experimentation.

What was your father's eyesight like?
He wore glasses for most of his adult life. They were large '70s-style frames that suited his larger than average head. There were points in the '80s when they'd broken and, unable to afford a new pair, he'd patched up the frames with Sellotape. The piece that is placed between both glasses and rests on the nose – the bridge! – was constantly falling out. When he was drunk he'd take them

off, the effect of which – along with the copious amounts of vodka – gave him an appearance of scowling through a dark tunnel. A suitable image for life.

And how ...
Sorry, just one more thing on the glasses : he had a pair of prescription sunglasses that he used for driving, John Lennon-style, though they were much bigger, their lenses thick black discs – like tarred medieval coins.

And how is your eyesight?
Worsening. I have prescription glasses for long-distance, though as I choose not to drive this means I don't wear them daily. They are essential for watching subtitled films. At the moment of writing I have a piece of gold or silver glitter lodged behind my left eye. It got accidentally trapped after my son was making an anti-ghost spray for which glitter was an essential ingredient.

Is it painful?
Intermittently. The pain recurs every hour or so : a feeling of someone forcing the back of my eye with a sharp implement.

And yet you're still able to write?
Should I not be able to? Joyce continued towards blindness through traumatic and worsening pain. In 1925 (three years after *Ulysses* was published) he had his seventh eye operation. Gordon Bowker, in *James Joyce: A New Biography*, describes him at this point as 'unable to see lights, suffering continual pain from the operation,

weeping oceans of tears, highly nervous, and unable to think straight. He was now dependent on kind people to see him across the road and hail taxis for him. All day, he lay on a couch in a state of complete depression, wanting to work but quite unable to do so.'

Did this have an impact on his writing?
The body can't be separated from the working processes of any person. Joyce would scrawl down tiny notes using a magnifying glass, as if watching tiny insects organise themselves towards a Dadaist revolution. It's been pointed out that the biggest invention in Joyce's writing is in the sound of the words : the 'Sirens' episode of *Ulysses*, for example, pushes language sound and by doing so challenges the idea of logical meaning : *By Bachelor's walk jogjaunty jingled Blazes Boylan, bachelor, in sun, in heat, mare's glossy rump atrot, with flick of whip, on bounding tyres : sprawled, warmseated, Boylan impatience, ardentbold. Horn. Have you the? Horn. Have you the? Haw haw horn.* This was all a warm-up for the all-out punnilingus of *Finnegans Wake* : speak the book aloud and it starts to live. Get your tongue around that.

And as we talk where are Stephen and Bloom now, 18th June 1904 at 2.48am?
Stephen is on Sandymount Strand watching Hamlet dig his own grave, after which he will have no choice but to return to the tower. Bloom is at home, once more top-to-toe with Molly. He is hoping to resurrect the conversation with her in the morning about touring with Stephen and cancelling her trip with Boylan on Monday. He feels

confident that he can convince the young poet to resume his singing career. Bloom himself will manage this tour, ensuring further companionship from Stephen whilst being at his wife's side each day. Molly will, of course, fall in love with him all over again and conceive another child.

And what will Stephen's response be?
That will be revealed in the sequel to *Dedalus*.

How is Stephen right now?
Drunk again, and becoming drunker : he has a carafe of red wine with him on the beach. He will wake on the morning of 18th June with a hangover. Fortunately for him it will be a Saturday. He will be in no mood for the face of Bloom and certainly not Mulligan and Haines. Between the sighting of the drowned man on the beach and the further sightings of the ghost of his mother and Hamlet he will have no patience for any further complications. We also need to remember that he has fallen in love, amidst this maelstrom of emotion, with the young woman he met earlier today. In short he is fucked with conflicting emotions.

Do his feelings for this young woman run deeper than the desire for unpaid sexual gratification? Are these feelings any different from the attraction he might also feel towards Molly Bloom?
If we were using Jung's stages of *anima* to measure Stephen's attitudes towards the two women – Molly and the younger woman – then the older woman might be classed as inciting the *Helen* stage (successful if not alto-

gether virtuous) which is only one stage above the *Eve* of the whores; the young girl would be whiter, undoubtedly in the *Mary* category (virtuous), bordering on the highest order : *Sophia*, capable of bringing from Stephen a sense that she might not only be some kind of Goddess but might possibly be one beyond that : a fully formed human being. As you can guess from this both Jung's and Stephen's attitudes towards women are questionable to say the least.

Why in your book does Stephen fall in love with this woman when Joyce himself based his novel on the specific date of 16th June 1904 because that was the day he first went out with Nora Barnacle?

Joyce based his novel on that day because that was a day that changed his life. However, the story of the relationship that began that day does not feature in his novel. Stephen is not in love with Nora Barnacle (though Joyce suggests that the intellectual tower Stephen lives inside was a cold and distant place that the love of the earthy Barnacle would shatter) and I have indulgently picked up the fictional element of Stephen and imagined a different encounter.

What would have given this girl *Sophia* status?

The reading of ancient philosophy and a favouring for Aristotle above Plato. A propensity to push back at his self-absorbed melancholia in a way that Ophelia is incapable of : allowing him to feel self-consciously like Hamlet, and thus draw him from the actual doppelgänger of the Danish Prince that he believes he is in conflict with.

And what about your own claims on *Hamlet*?
By which you mean?

Every youngish man of a certain intellect wants to play the Prince.
I once looked at the clouds and gave them names.

Which names?
Nimbostromuscumulicirrusstreakedsalmonpuffs.

You were trying to become a poet?
Trying to become a poet is like trying to get past St Peter as a Fedex courier.

How long have you spoken in metaphors?
Since my symbolics dropped.

What, art a heathen? How dost thou understand the Scripture?
You speak the words of the First Clown. And that makes me?

The Second. What is he that builds stronger than either the mason, the shipwright, or the carpenter?
The gallows-maker; for that frame outlives a thousand tenants.

>   ENTER HAMLET AND HORATIO, AT
>   A DISTANCE.

Do you see them?
Yes, I was awaiting his reappearance back in the narrative. Stephen is expecting him too. Ah for fuck's sake, I can't take any more of this …

Would you like to speak to him?
I've taken a vow never to speak to my heroes. Hamlet permeated my teens. I wanted his experience as I wanted to own the mind of Stephen. I created my own personal mythology out of these characters, fusing in the working class ethics of Arthur Seaton from *Saturday Night and Sunday Morning*.

A figure some way distant from the sophistry of Dedalus?
I drank a lot and wanted an intellectual licence to do so. I was comfortable inside the avatar of both men; I was not quite as intellectual as Stephen but more sensitive than Seaton. It was good for me that I didn't discover the work and life of Malcolm Lowry until many years later … can we exit this – digression – here – I actually need a strong drink quite badly …

What's the matter now?
I've lost the thread. I have a book to write. Can we please get on with it?

You only had to say the word.

PENELOPE

*Act 5, Scene 2: A hall in the castle /
Sandymount Strand. 2.48am*

No. So much for this. What follows tannins is absence of liquid. The absinthe has stripped me. My mother's outline a husk : her name the only fact. After the pandybat I pined for her. Nice mother. The miles between us disappeared in the thought of her smile. That absence now a vacuum she pulls me towards. Will I go? Wait and she comes to me : Gertrude in lace. In my heart there has been fighting that will not let me sleep.

Was the baldman my Polonius? Behind the arras I let him pass. I see this sea as my shawl : *arrasarras*. He played no part in my plot, I could not pull him back. *aratarat*. My Rosencrantz and Guildenstern were on the ramparts. Adders fanged. Return? I cannot.

I will undress here. Skeins of cotton and lesser fabrics. Corpsewhite my flesh is : the descendant of my mother. Why do I? Unclean. More than this : to be cleansed is more than to be clean. Leave the trousers here : Mulligans. Let the sea take them. Let them wash to the Muglins. Such bugs and goblins I must peel off from my life.

Must wash. Will I feel cleaner in this darkness? There's another light on the tower in the sea : it roves like the eye of the cyclops. It takes me it leaves me it takes me it leaves me. The sea annuls the lice. A statement of self : from the spoors life grows. I could see Bloom's disapproval, smell his scent of florid lemon. His wife a succubus : take me in thy bosom. Molly flounders. I've seen her about town with a man, brazen and ruddy with greed. A non-thinker : ferment and think later. A propagator of whole armies.

A louse. How many like this in my hair? Water, wonder if … Floats. No upthrusting Eureka! for this. No nakedness outside the cortex. His futile legs claw the tide : dust mote in a sandstorm. A chrysalis I found here as a child. *Dargida procinctus* : nightmoth. An inch under sand it slept then I dug it up to light. Prebirth. The cocoon moved of its own accord. Expectations of colours, the mind races in sequins and wingbuntings.

If the ghost would have called me this morning would I have followed? The Dane did : do I not set my life by his pin's fee? Remember the skull of the *Homo erectus* in the museum. Its cheek a cracked ceramic. Two yellow teeth on a dish beside it : woodchips. The loose change of a spent life.

Light flickers. A bobbingblackboat imprisoned by the sea it was built for. All land is its harbour. A peagreen boat unmoored, wrapped-up in an old five pound note. The owl plays lookout for the pussycat.

Will I continue to perform for myself? Socrates asked questions because he questioned the accuracy of the oracle. My questions are ingrown : is there anyone in Dublin who can clip these from me? Her perhaps. She is the one my mind holds so many versions of, not all decent enough to be played back to her. Free me from this catastrophic loom.

A form in the distance. Can it be a man? Head and shoulders grown from the sand? A whole body submerged. I will circle, play fox to this sparrow.

Plato banished Homer because Homer saw both good and evil in the Gods. I see both too. Will the Society of Vice let me pass the gates? St Peter stands where I need a Priapus. My language has a virus and feeds on past ages.

Look : lugworm. A vortex of coiled sand : a fossil for the night. Will I transform into characters of my own making? The future me I mean : the one I am yet to become. I will occupy the imagined self I never was. When I return they will treat me like a priest or a giver of pleasure and tell me I have no place in their city. I will leave for faroff shores : annointed with myrhh and crowned with briars.

The sun brings growth and light : the power of seeing. The Good, Reality and Truth. Am I double-blinded? The tide recedes : takes the evidence in its muddy bride's whites.

I see clearer now : it is he, Hamlet, the hero of that other book. What does he dig for? A grave made out of sand. An hourglass he stands inside, his ears in outraged mutiny. Should I make comparison? Perhaps all will be well after all, no two heroes die at once. I am Fortinbras then?

Well I am not. Yesterday was an uneventful day. Today I have vomited on a dead man, been pursued by the ghost of my mother and experienced a married man trying to pair me with his wife in name of song. And fallen in love.

He digs before me. Grains fall from his spade. His limbs ache as time falls away from him. I will watch where he does not see, blinded by the Cyclops. Each muse I've lavished has been the shadow cast from a flame and a sheet. I have grown accustomed to their forms. Their voices are not their own. Their movements hinged with rosewood. My eyes are well used to halflight. Now I see by the sun : Plato equates this with Good. A new self mutates in the fleshrot? No, the same. I chased my own ideal along cobbled streets. Closed my eyes and prayed to open them on new experience. My hands have levied all physical things and now I've seen her. I see the cave I've lived in. If she was to yield then at last I could write.

These waves unharness my feet. What is on the other shore is the reality I must face, my body must move to understand what it means. My contemporaries are animals cut from wood. Now I've seen real flesh can I return? Day vision may be beyond me but the sun is outside the cave. Her eyes : hewn rosewood. If she was to come I would go.

The Bard left his secondbest bed with the dried stains of a wedding night. No sound like the sad springs of rejection. Echoes of the act that is no more. Bloom grieves his Hamnet. Would I step into the vortex of this sadness? Another woman I have seen now : supple and sealithe. Is she the mermaid that lures me away from frustration? One look unlocks the eunuch's loss.

Am I the coat of the man I will be? Entelechy : I will fulfill what I set out do. In ten years, a novel. And poetry? Should any fiction be without? Shakespeare's oeuvre is a double helix of iambics and characters. What he made is living within me. Good writers make books, the genius creates epics. I can't take the music from my epic. I won't look back when I leave the underworld. My lyre is in my ear.

My father sees my flight as insult. He stands drinks while I steal library slips. I will not be on loan from him. If I sing, as Artifoni says, I am just his ghost. My music must be encased in metrics.

That riddle I set yesterday, what was its purpose? A fox burying its grandmother? The ruse of familial nouns : maternal bones pocked with skin. The tang of the whore has thrown off the scent. The fox in my head scratches the lodestone of wisdom.

The sea is just as Algy said it was : a great sweet mother. Malachi misses the swish of this music. His meat is human flesh. Swinburne's name a mnemonic for the sound of seawaves. He was both alcoholic and algolagniac : his pleasures sourced his pain. His mother a male literary critic, cockling up warm milk in a mansion in Putney. Ths crtc, wh s t? Wtts-Dntn, sndpc f *Th thnm*. H ddrsss th pt s Th Brd ndr thr wn rf. Slpprs nd pp wth thr npstc chttr. wndr f thy'r n rrrs t thr mlkwmn?

[RECEIVING TEXT]

Disappointed met *A Channel Passage* but who else has the dexterous lilt of the somnambulent line? That fierce patter of monosyllabic shrapnel. *Glad mad night sank panting and satiate.* And it's the sea in his work, the sea, beyond any living poet. Perhaps there lies the test : even when landlocked the true poet hears the sea's music cascade through their bloodpulse? *The keen waves kindled and quickened as things transfigured or things distraught.* What could he conjure from these turning tides at night?

The fey grasshopper, Yeats, is of the past. He wants his swan to be more than swan. Another of Plato's students. Who will show us the world of objects in verse? The oculus in reverse? This must be my rôle. This handful of sand in darkness is still sand : it does not transform because each grain can't be seen. So with language : the sound as significant as what it signifies. Yeats' latest release expands in linelengths but does his advice on long love resonate? He has that one advantage over me, the rest I can teach him.

Was A.E. right that those *things* are too vague? Shadowy forms with no hook in the world of ideals? But what does his own verse show us : hermetic homes of the heart pulasting in alternating endrhymes. His knowledge rattles inside an empty nut, his visions are not for alltime. They live a day on this famished isle. Caliban in catalectics. A slip of Shelley's sublime.

If A.E. was a better poet would I have spent his loan on the whore? I must pay back the poets in shoelaces. Leonard's ... Bloom's riffling of Shakespeare for life advice : a calendar of catastrophes. Thought I would never shake him off at St. Stephen's Green. Perhaps she was perched for the bedtrick? I must not grieve : my gift lures me overseas.

This starfish : sensate they say it is. It bristles even though it is blind beyond its five points. An intricate web of nerves that learns from touch. Will I see the whore again? I paid her with A.E.'s money. And with the potfund from the education of children. Today I am spent. Tomorrow?

My schooling no different. A boy I knew, Aubrey Mills, while the others took sticks he carried a lamp and a whistle. Sirens and lights : he drew me to a world beyond the blade. I close my eyes and see his face. Open. Buoy lights. Coruscation across the waves. The world distracts from the forms I hold within : they are not beyond this world. They frame my portrait.

Heron : another schoolfriend. Both symbol and legislator of his name. Perched for the kill. Asked me about Eileen under the Chinese lanterns. Whipped my calves with the cane until I spoke. *Confessio*, he said. Was I the smallfry to his maximus? I yielded. Escape came from that. And Ireland? I did the same. Will do again? Whip my flesh and I speak. Escape? I think not. The torque of the lash follows. I will create my *magnum opus* from the flashwounds.

Defecation follows comprehension. Where will I go? What if he sees me? Over bindweed and sheep rope I walk. Past the broken hull to the cove. Must watch my step : Xenocrates tripped in the night and drowned in a cistern.

Here will do. The beast with one back. If she could see me now? Between the gate and the cave, ideal love disperses. She too : red roses are not so red. Don't like to think : keep the muse from the worm. Dehydration binding : mustn't overforce. I have windblocked my own flow. Lubriciousness would be welcome. Perhaps a woman could fortify against this darkness. Feed me fruit and whisper of the olive grove. A seachange, yes : the final Act. It runs from me in pools of small fish. I piss it too. What is solid and what is wet is beyond me. Inseparable from sand but darker : insoluble. Must wash. The sea's toilette. Lemon and springwater.

Would I take Leonard's wife? Bronzebreasted and amplethighed. Did she sleep while I trespassed her house? And Bloom, alert to my lust. Better me than his adversary : the chafed brute of the nonthinker. There's no horn as sharp as that of a singer. Throatsong spurred by gonads. And to think of me back then : all smiles and questions in my Fauntleroy blazer.

The *Symposium* begins with drink, the *Republic* with questions. Afterthought and riposte. Each day's probing ends with serifs, reaches towards matins. The chair of the discussion has two legs, not four : language extends the form. Exists in a world of multiples. A choir of coincidences.

My father's school desk was etched with *foetus* : was I just an echo set forth from his ample shoulders? They joshed each other towards conformity, each believing themselves unique. Write the word and the thing is born. For me the wood is the word, and the word the craft to make things : I will multiply through art. I must make and by making find myself. Will my father find me here? Horatio I will not believe is outside the true avouch of mine own eyes. He tries to compel me to act : I do not rise. If he is no King I, too, am no Prince.

Aristotle dried out his dandyism with overthought. Love, it was, Hermias's concubine : a girl called Pythias. Love rushed through the logic of the palace. Where was the ideal then? Ah, the girl herself : an idea and a mortal face. She had known men before and he had crawled that floor many times. Thirty-seven he was, she eighteen. Her age, at the gate? The same.

Love's bitter mystery. Do I feel it twice? What else was in my mother's drawer? A wooden rosary, rose oil, a sketch of my ghostself made when I was six. A pink living thing in a starched blacksuit. The yellow wheel of the yo-yo in my pocket. I made counting rhymes as it climbed. A poet to a wheel : I must break the set rhythms.

The tower is my *omphalos*. Wll thr b wngd wrds frm th Gds? Thnk nt. Th mlkwmn's lbtns wll trn dly mr gry. Mld f Thrn nd slnd : rtfcts my frbrs fnd frm th Stn g. [RECEIVING TEXT] The Sirens call and the Muglins batter their heartbeats. I will be stormwashed as I leave. Leander : I tie myself to your bosom.

What was it Haines said : are you a believer *in the narrow sense of the word?* What narrow channel could there be to God? Clip the choirs of the Seraphim and crawl like a worm wrapped in a dampened scroll.

Hamlet speaks. To me?

– Dost know this water-fly? –

I must answer. Walk towards. Not too much, enough to …

– Dost thou know this water-fly?

– I don't know what you mean …

He throws a book. I must. The poems of Yeats.

– Yes, I know him. He is too old to learn from me.

He digs like his bones are down there. What must he? A skull, dusted with loam. A feminine turn to his hips : an androgyny that well suits the skeleton.

– This, Stephen, is the skull of your mother. I want you to take it.
– How did my mother come to be here? I cannot see! We buried her beneath ground, inside wood.
– There's a divinity that shapes our ends. Take it … What she was is not was she is. Woman's constant. Now take it.

I cannot pick it up. Can I leave? The sea must have it, smooth its seesaw edges with spume. He disappears in his own grave : the actions of his life determine an eternity. I no longer have the key. I will sleep here, expunge the ghost of the drowned man.

The silver mane of Manannán plunders for my feet. All colour is made by light, is the sea the same? I feel its pull yet in dark I fear it. I stand here no more with a bucket and a question. I recall the sermon on Hell, he who raised a hand against his father would be cast in a seasack : with a cock, a monkey and a serpent.

On that shore I'll be at a further point of remove. When I am closed to the ineluctable modalities I will see the city for what it is. Shimmering city by the sea simmering ceaselessly.

Will I capture the appearance or the reality? I must go fishing in pure thought and surface with objects true to their form.

My knowledge is my craftsmanship : both validate my Dublin. A shoemaker dragging his laces through ink. If the music dilutes from my prose I'll need a fishwife with a textblock. It is the player's extempore scenes that show reality. Black fish leap from a hot sea.

I take Plato's jibe : ban myself from the state. Poetry, he said, corrupts the best characters. I am the best character in this book : now Jamesy, lift me up, away from the interloping Prince. Away from this play within. I killed my mother with silence and sincerity. Would my father take a second lover? Who would have him? His mortal frame forever charred with her ashes. I have this feeling that another authors me.

All sea ends in brown foam. Maks nw ch dy wht th sn drd t snd. Frtlss nd ftl xrcs. Wtch t btwn th clshng msc f pnts nd tlk. Ths lf s lqds ftr whch nly wrds rmn.

[RECEIVING TEXT]

The sea in cloisters of monksong sings for me, clatters its sibilants. No wave is the same : like words their song is strung with combinations. To listen is to play. Tufts of weedroots flounce to the tide's waveloom. The lost pate of the deadman? His toupée attached to the sea's tight chest. His eyes enraged by his hairless secret. At least his loincloth was in place. No tiddling bream to broach the faces of his clapless audience. Would I die like this? Lie down and let the sea take me to further shores? Watch the crowds watch helpless. There goes Stephen : he was once Chrysostomos.

Poolbeg Lighthouse : its signature beam of white every fifteen seconds. Its purpose not to look but to be seen. You can feel what it is to be watched : a mote in the eye of the Cyclops. Its purpose to fend men from the rocks, not to lure them. Yet it brings me here. Could I sleep inside? Tonight this sand. Let them find me in fleshfolds of disappointment. Disappointment is my calling.

This empty can : I will listen. The sound of myself. Since I was a child I've been occupied with hidden messages : from the sea, from the other. I fear I can hear at last. Her heartbeat drums trochaically in my ears. The constant rut of another's dagger.

He in black surfaces again, speaks to me :

– I loved her, from that I can't escape –
– What will this digging into sand achieve?
– An end to all of this. We measure our lives in such grains until there is only darkness left around us.
– You will dig until the end?
– No. This is the end. Do you love another?
– Today I felt a change : I met her at the gates of the beach.
– And what will you do to show your love for her?
– To show my love?
– Would you take one of these?

A shower of knives he throws : stand back! Yesterday began with a razor and a mirror now French rapiers and poniards lay crossways on the sand.

– Choose your weapon from them.
– I will not die on these shores.
– What then, to England?
– Europe.
– And your love?
– She must come with me.
– You may win at the odds.

Ach, his heart takes the blade : his eyes are as blacked as the racing squid. Is he dead? Hamlet is no more. He lies in this bed he has made for himself, the tide will tuck him in. Shadow of Shakespeare's son, more real to me than my own father. And me? I will make an eiderdown from this sand.

What a son am I that can so astonish a mother? Astonish her to death. I would not let her fade. Is this why sh fllws?

[RECEIVING TEXT]

My mother's skull is found and Hamlet is dead. I will walk through mudflats to the lighthouse. Let the doctor and Englishman join the Dane in sleep. The lighthouse is above them all. The waves lather the rocks at Dublin Bay. Words will come then : the beginnings of my real work. Yes, to the lighthouse : let the sand suck me towards its inner circles. The sea measures my purpose with its ruthlessness. The light that blinds me is also the light that steers me. T t e ligh o e.

N mre wll sh walk ths shre wth hr gldn mthd sn.

[RECEIVING TEXT]

And will it end?
In a world of possibles.
Perhaps.

MAPS : PART III

Another room in the castle /
  St. Stephen's Green *215*

Another room in the castle /
  the dressing-room of Sarah Bernhardt *216*

A churchyard / The mind of Chris McCabe *217*

A hall in the castle / Sandymount Strand *218*

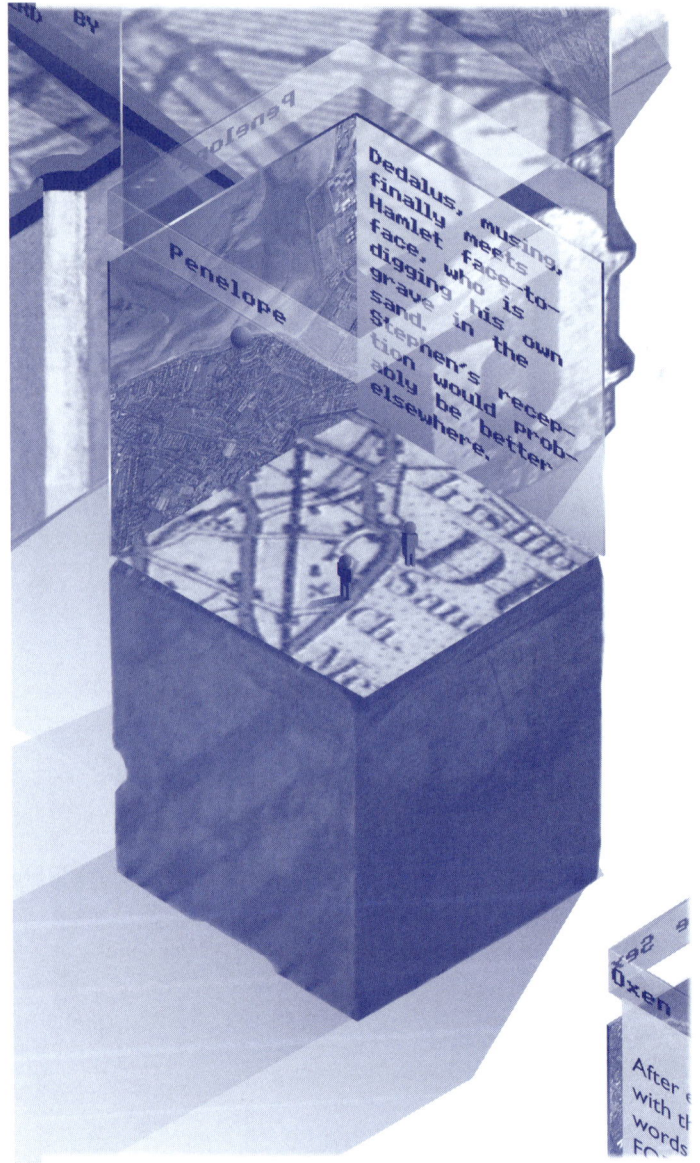

NOTES

TELEMACHUS : As Harry Shortlock has pointed out in issue 14 of *Hypermedia Joyce Studies*, Stephen may well be rattled by the onset of a new ABC: the The Atanasoff-Berry Computer, which would initiate many of the basic principles of computing. The feeling of being duplicated, transported and filed as a digital entity is on many levels similar to a hangover. This glitch can readily be translated as 'agenbite of inwit', explaining how Stephen misremembers Bloom's name as 'Leonard'. 'So here we find Stephen', Shortlock writes, 'the man, the myth, the block of clearly-defined pixels.'

NESTOR : Known for dispensing his expertise with superciliousness, and unpredictable results, Nestor was among the first to offer technical support for the Acorn Archimedes computing model of 1987. The Acorn was subject to a number of computing errors which Sue Jenkins, in the *The Glitching World of Ulysses*, has written, 'now becomes endemic to this scrambled, disorderly and flawed sequel – if we can even call it that.' The demand placed on the programme here makes the text to glitch, allowing Voltimand and Cornelius from *Hamlet* to walk through the episode.

PROTEUS : And what about Nora, you might ask? Joyce set *Ulysses* on 16th June 1904, though his mirror self Stephen falls for no woman in that *lingua mundi*. Nora is Molly! someone shouts. In fact in this episode Nora has been transformed to an all too literal artefact; a barnacle. Joyce, near-blind, <Rtn> to the beach and sorts crustacea like lost buttons, while Stephen <Esc> sets about falling in love for himself.

CALYPSO : In the early 1980s Frankin developed the Apple 1000 clone, a replica of the Apple II+, sold on the market as competition to the original Apple product. In 1988 Apple won a lawsuit over Franklin who was outlawed from making any further 'clone' machines.

LOTUS EATERS : Remember when 'surfing the net' meant an unwelcome onslaught of advertising pop-ups? By now we are feeling that. Patrick Killaney in *Ulysses: the Book that Lived Online Before it was Printed* makes a strong argument that Bridie Keller, the first woman (a prostitute) that Bloom had sex with is in fact hacking the text here. As a result the scene crashes with an advertisement for a skin lotion. Cookies are an essential part of a crash-diet. Maybe if Bloom had deleted some he wouldn't end up so hungry in chapter nine.

```
Sweny?s Pharmacy Directions.
Choose starting point, or click on the map.
>GOTO 51
```

HADES : Who is the man in the mackintosh? What does he carry inside that coat? Does the man in the mackintosh use an Apple Macintosh? Arthur Simons in his work *The Book that Cloned a Thousand Books* employs forensic typography to argue that the man in the mackintosh uses a Compac Portable. This is unlikely. The Macintosh Portable was heavy, weighing sixteen pounds, and expensive (US$6,500). But at last, 70 years after the 1.4lb 1922 edition (350 F for the signed copies; 250 F for the vergé d'Arches copies and 150 F for the remaining 750), Apple had introduced a truly portable computer. But could the man in the macintosh really fit this under his mackintosh?

```
There?s a man outside in a long coat, grey hat,
smoking a cigarette.
>GOTO 59
```

AEOLUS : Wind is prevalent here, or is it just Microsoft Word crashing again before saving the essential doc? In Act 3, scene 2 of *Hamlet*, King Claudius wonders whether Hamlet's love for Ophelia might well be the cause of his madness. Meanwhile Hamlet proves with algebra whether it is better 'to be or not to be', $(2b > -2b)$

This is more difficult to resolve than at first appears. If the goal of the equation were to return to 0 (to die, to sleep), then $2b > 0$ depends on the value of b (life) which could of course be negative (weary life). The *A-level Algebra Guide : Hamlet* suggests the famous soliloquy would oscillate endlessly between -2b and 2b, introducing negative and positive values of b, if this alternating current did not turn awry, returning Hamlet to action. Their potential difference quickens this 'so long life'. Resolution is no longer a sickly 72, but a print-ready 300dpi. The past is like a PDF. Uneditable.

What do you read, my lord? Hamlet was asked. Word, Word, Word. Will Bloom and Molly ever have another child after Rudy's death?

```
Are you ready to recover?
>GOTO 67
```

LESTRYGONIANS : The annoying thing about the current Davy Byrne's pub is that you can only get a gorgonzola sandwich and burgundy at a weekend. *Ulysses* was set on a Thursday. How dare they determine our movements like this? It brings to mind those first online banner ads of 1994 which said: 'Have you ever clicked your mouse right here? YOU WILL.'

maps/search/dublin+ireland+restaurants
>GOTO 71

SCYLLA AND CHARYBDIS : Every attempt has been made to cut-and-paste Stephen's exact credentials from *Ulysses* into *Dedalus* without loss: the slim frame, the ashplant, the borrowed trousers. Something, of course, may have slipped from the clipboard. In this section his poem has been created through a simple process of finding (and replacing) all the uses of 'Denmark' in *Hamlet* with 'Dublin'. Critics would be right to question the false reality of Stephen achieving this so quickly in his notebook. On his chromebook, however, it took just seconds.

```
Here, you?ve left your poem on the desktop...
>GOTO 79
```

WANDERING ROCKS : 'I think I may have seen you on MySpace' Bloom said to Stephen. 'That's an obsolete platform', Stephen replied. AOL Messenger seemed like a breakthrough at the time. Stephen naturally recoils from likefollowlikefollowlikefollow. Bloom signs up to LinkedIn to look for freelance advertising work.

```
Are you sure you want to move these 19 items
to the Recycle Bin?
>GOTO 87
```

SIRENS : Arnold Asquith in *James Joyce: The Man Who Heard Thunder in Every Nut* argues that the sound poem was invented by Hugo Ball at the Cabaret Voltaire in 1916. There is a picture of Ball wearing a faux-metal suit just like the Tin Man in *The Wizard of Oz*. Asquith is right to point out that the opening poem in this section is an overture of the corresponding 'Sirens' episode in *Ulysses* – although here the sound of the text is that of Bloom urinating in a public toilet at Temple Bar. Each section of this version of 'Sirens' recycles the language of the sections of *Dedalus* up until this point. Déjà vu? 'There is a strong narrative drive in each poem here', Asquith writes and then goes on to detail the action of each poem: Bloom zipping up his trousers; Bloom whistling; coins rattling in Bloom's trousers; the sound of a trumpet; Bloom throwing cash to a busker; a literal gust of wind; the bells of the church sounding out Bloom's happiness in the thought that Molly might join him and Stephen on a British tour; a seagull soaring over the Liffey and Bloom's double-checking that he has Molly's lotion in his pocket. In a classroom in Hull I once workshopped Hugo Ball's poem with primary school children. I asked them if the picture of Ball reminded them of anyone – expecting them to say the Tin Man. A hand went up. 'Yes!' I said. 'Is it you sir?' the child asked.

```
No cover disk? Ask your newsagent.
>GOTO 95
```

CYCLOPS : 'Cyclops is a computer system co-invented by the British inventor Bill Carlton of Great Britain and Margaret Parnis England of Malta, which is used on the ATP and WTA professional tennis tours as an electronic line judge to help determine whether a serve is in or out.

The system, which must be activated by the service line umpire before each serve, projects five or six infra-red horizontal beams of light along the court 10 mm above the ground. One beam covers the good (short) side of the service line and others cover the fault (long) side. If a served ball hits the first beam, the other beams are turned off, while a long serve will break one of the other beams. A long serve is indicated by an audible signal. Obvious long serves that go beyond Cyclops' beams are called by the service line umpire. The system is tuned before and during each tournament by a representative of the company which rents the system. This representative stays through the tournament and confers with tournament officials afterwards to determine any problems which may have arisen. The system has been constantly refined to improve accuracy, although no statistics on its efficacy are available.

The Cyclops computer system was introduced to the Wimbledon Championships in 1980 and the U.S. Open in 1981, and was also used at the Australian Open. In 2007 it was removed from Wimbledon's Centre Court and Court No. 1 to allow the use of the Hawk-Eye system first introduced at the U.S. Open in 2006. At the present time Cyclops is not used in any capacity at any of the Grand Slam events.

A famous moment involving Cyclops occurred at Wimbledon in 1980 when Ilie Năstase got down on his hands and knees to talk to the equipment to argue an 'out' signal.' [Source: Wikipedia, accessed 10 Dec 2017]

```
Report "@CitizenCyclops", How is this Tweet abu-
sive or harmful?

?It directs hate against a protect category (e.g,
race, religion, gender, orientation, disability)
>REBOOT
>GOTO 95
```

NAUSICAA : Many critics have pointed out Joyce's interest in pornography and his fetish for watching women urinate. Anna Livia Plurabelle was washed like a fontanelle, dispersed water like a plumber. In this section the priest masturbates whilst watching Bloom, who is walking to the Martello Tower to find Stephen.

Andy McPherson in his multi-volume *The Beady Eye Behind the Lens* has contextualised the Victorian pornography market that the mind of Leopold Bloom emerged from. Perhaps in his life before the internet Bloom would have read such titillating titles as *The Power of Mesmerism: A Highly Erotic Narrative (1891)*, *The Seducing Cardinal (1830)*, *The Lustful Turk (1864)*, *Captain Stroke-All's Pocket Book! (1844)*, *An Experimental Lecture by Colonel Spanker (1878)*, and *The Amatory Experiences of a Surgeon (1881)*. Such readers also wouldn't want to miss *The Autobiography of a Flea (1887)* and *Revelries! and Devilries!! (1867)*.

The latter has a lascivious frontispiece showing two naked women with birches ready to lash a pair of bare buttocks.

```
Can I get virgin media in my area?
>REFRESH
>GOTO 95
```

OXEN OF THE SUN : Loom and Babbage both used incredibly limited languages. In *Stephen Dedalus and the Invention of the Human Internet* Matthew Sinclair argues that without the transfer of Stephen into more orthogonal semantic and syntactical routines the invention of a more recursive typing system with higher-order functions would not have been possible. It's down to this process of transferring a semi-fictional poet into data that we have seen the development of assembly languages, short codes, machine codes, compilers and autocodes. This has now allowed Dedalus to prove by algebra that Hamlet's grandson is Shakespeare's grandfather and that he himself is the ghost of his own father. This could not have happened without C++, Visual Basic and Java. Loom. Babbage.

```
George Saintsbury?s Specimens of English CSS.
>GOTO 119
```

CIRCE : Novels can exist without a subconscious but they die without an id. Excess leads to the paid-for counselling session. I should know. Every Analyst has been Analyzed (though not all have been Optimized). Every chef needs to eat. Do we know where the patient and professional begin and end? (Think of the perineum). Can this book be cured? The clock is ticking, and the going rate for an hour's therapy in Dublin is 80 euros.

```
Error 404 : You are in D4. Try turning yourself
off and on again.
>GOTO 137
```

EUMAEUS : Is the omniscient narrator an interruptive jarvey? Is he a wolf in sheep's clothing? A wall behind a hallway's bunting? A breeze in a sailor's anorak? A fox in a taxi's wheel arch? A maggot in a crow's craw? A snail in the gutter's sliproad? A stencil in a cartographer's selection box? An eye in a blind man's pick 'n' mix? An apple in a farmer's Lexus? An asterisk in a guarantor's small print? A pickle in a civil servant's handbag? A bauble in the Easter Bunny's wicker? A boxing glove in a ballerina's treasure chest? A battery in the maneki-neko's base? A tattoo in the blue ghost's craft box? A Tamagotchi in the city's aftermath? A bullet in a tropical fish tank? A banknote in the trumpet's neck? A dragonfly at the priest's window? A pump in the widow's wardrobe? A flugelhorn in the policeman's retinue? A dicky bow in the undertaker's pocket? A sock in the hand of an urban planner? A straw in the mouth of a scarecrow? A pea on the ledge of a doll's house? A sparrow on the dancefloor of a turntable? A meme in the mind of a taxidermist? A tick in the eye of the newsagent? A bit in the banker's data plan? A blot.

ITHACA : On being asked 'Why do you always answer a question with a question?' the only logical answer is 'What do you mean?'

PENELOPE : Readers should have a monthly data package of at least 4GB before embarking on this section. While Bloom weights in at an average of 3.5mb per section, Dedalus weighs in here at a massive 7.6mb. Those with intermittent broadband connection may experience some level of disruption, especially when Dedalus at last comes face-to-face with Hamlet, who turns out to be another bit string of no insubstantial substance. As the action here takes place at 2am you could always try hacking your neighbour's WiFi. Who itemises their internet bill these days?

ACKNOWLEDGEMENTS

The first draft of this book was written between 2013 and 2014 during which time I taught a course for The Poetry School called The Bloomsday Project. I'm grateful to all of the students on that course for the close reading, ideas and conversation throughout. I'll always remember our Bloomsday performance in the Blue Elephant theatre in Camberwell on 16th June 2014.

I am also grateful to the Bluecoat in Liverpool for facilitating funding through the Liverpool-Ireland Cultural Corridor (LICC), thanks go to Adam Smythe, Marie-Anne McQuay and Bryan Biggs. I'd also like to thanks Jonathan Creasy for showing me around the James Joyce Centre in October 2015.

Sections of this book were first published in *The Dedalus Poems*, Openings-Closings Press, 2015, with thanks to Bernard Moxham. The Aeolus page was included in *The New Concrete: Visual Poetry in the 21st Century* (2015), thanks to my co-editor Victoria Bean and Hayward Publishing.

I'd like to thank Max Porter for detailed feedback and enthusiasm for an early draft of this book, and for the cover blurb. Max you were right when you said someone would publish this book and do it well, and that person is David Henningham. David has been a companion in the realms of experimental fiction for many years, and our wading through the work of B.S. Johnson has been influential on *Dedalus*. Thank you David for the excitement and generative collaboration on this book, for pushing me to write the notes and then responding with the maps. We've made a whole world around and in addition to the core of the novel. It has been a huge joy for me.

Other people who have encouraged my writing over the years and made their mark on these pages in some way are Tom Chivers, my editor at Penned in the Margins; Sophie Herxheimer for enthusiasm in our studio time; my *Debris* comrades Simon Barraclough and Isobel Dixon; Pascal O'Loughlin for reading my earlier fiction and pushing experimental writers my way, from New Narrative to George Bataille. Finally my brother Ste whose approach to his music for the past 20 years has been influential in its DIY work ethic.

My dad played a huge part in passing on his *The Essential James Joyce* to me over twenty years ago.

This novel wouldn't have been possible without the love, patience and encouragement of my wife Sarah who kept everything together while I was off amassing words ('Dad's off on tour or in a meeting…'). So many lemon soaps for you my Ness! And all my love to Pavel too for your enthusiasm for Joyce's language, a big 'Mrkgnao!' to you my lad.

HENNINGHAM FAMILY PRESS

Find more Henningham Family Press publications at : *henninghamfamilypress.co.uk*

All our paperback fiction is reinterpreted in our studio, with the author, as limited edition handmade Artists' Books.

Subscribers to Henningham Family Press receive all our paperback fiction at a discount, through their door on publication day.

Kunstverein subscribers receive one handmade limited edition as well. Find out how to subscribe on our website.

ABOUT THE AUTHOR

Chris McCabe was born at Mill Road Hospital in Liverpool in 1977, on the site of a Victorian workhouse. He is the author of four poetry collections, *The Hutton Inquiry, Zeppelins, THE RESTRUCTURE* (all with Salt Publishing) and, most recently, *Speculatrix* (Penned in the Margins) which was commended in the Forward Prize. He has recorded his work for the Poetry Archive and was shortlisted for The Ted Hughes Award in 2013 for his collaborative book with Maria Vlotides, *Pharmapoetica*.

He is also the author of a series of creative non-fiction books that aims to discover a great lost poet in one of London's Magnificent Seven cemeteries. This began in 2014 with *In the Catacombs: a Summer Among the Dead Poets of West Norwood Cemetery* (which was selected as an LRB Bookshop book of the year) and was followed in 2016 by *Cenotaph South: Mapping the Lost Poets of Nunhead Cemetery*. With Victoria Bean he is the co-editor of *The New Concrete: Visual Poetry in the 21st Century* (Hayward Publishing, 2015) and his own visual work can be found in *The Affairs of Dylan Thomas* (Red Fox Press, 2017), a series of collages, poetry collages and visual poems.

He works as the National Poetry Librarian at Southbank Centre's National Poetry Library and lives in Liverpool with his wife and son.